AFTER THE FIRE

TO: JUDY CORSER & GRACE GREEN

Who write wonderful books,
and without whose voices on
the telephone I would long since
have lost my sanity.

AFTER THE FIRE

BY
KAY GREGORY

MILLS & BOON LIMITED
ETON HOUSE   18–24 PARADISE ROAD
RICHMOND   SURREY   TW9 1SR

*First published in Great Britain 1993
by Mills & Boon Limited*

© Kay Gregory 1993

*Australian copyright 1993
Philippine copyright 1993
Large Print edition 1993*

ISBN 0 263 13421 0

*Set in Times Roman 16 on 17 pt.
16-9307-54697 C*

*Printed and bound in Great Britain by
William Clowes, Beccles, Suffolk.*

CHAPTER ONE

'STAND right there on the line, please. That's right, sir. Now *smile*.'

Richard didn't smile. He side-stepped neatly as the camera clicked open to capture a candid image of the unsuspecting passenger behind him.

A soft, deliciously feminine voice muttered, 'Rats!' and he glanced over his shoulder to see the owner of the voice hoisting two smart new suitcases and a shoulder-bag as she stumbled up the gangway towards him.

'Can I help?' he asked, as the staggering figure caught up to him. He reached for the nearest suitcase, anticipating grateful acceptance.

Two large brown eyes in a small, flower-like face looked up at him with quick suspicion as his hand brushed against hers. When she unwillingly relinquished the suitcase, he saw her catch her breath, and felt an unexpected flare of irritation.

5

'I don't bite,' he said crisply. 'But if you think I might, there *are* porters. I always use them myself.'

The young woman's face turned a soft, attractive pink. 'I'm sure you don't bite. And yes, I know about porters, thank you, but the one who offered to take my baggage before we boarded stood much too close to me—and he smelled of beer. I decided I could manage on my own.'

'I see,' said Richard, observing the determined tilt to the girl's small, pointed chin. 'But I assure you I don't drink beer for breakfast, and I have no immediate plans to stand too close. So I think you can safely trust me with your luggage.'

'Yes, of course. Thank you,' she agreed, but with a reluctance she wasn't quite able to conceal.

'Right.' He ignored the reluctance. 'Where's your cabin?'

'Deck Three, I think.'

A uniformed figure at the head of the gangway informed them smilingly that her cabin was indeed on Deck Three. Richard, unsmilingly, removed the other case from her unresisting grasp, tucked his briefcase under his arm, and made for the orange doors of the lift.

'What was all that about rats?' he asked, as the door slid closed behind them.

'What? What on earth are you talking about?' The small, turned-up nose in the pert little face was raised in puzzled enquiry, and Richard felt an instant stab of shock.

Of course. No wonder he'd felt drawn to this prickly young woman. Now that he thought about it, he had recognised at once that there was something all too familiar about that nose—and about the wide curving mouth and the short curls bouncing on her neck... He smoothed a hand over his jaw and gave her neat figure a slow and thorough appraisal. She ignored him and stared woodenly ahead at the doors.

Hmm. She was smaller than he would have expected. Not beautiful by any standards, but there was something very appealing about her. Always had been, as he remembered, although she seemed to be as suspicious of him now as she had been the last time they met. Just as well she hadn't recognised him yet...

He strummed his fingers lightly on his thigh. It would take six days for *Supership III* to sail from New York to Southampton. Six days that in the suspended reality of life on board ship could seem a lifetime. Perhaps after eleven months he was ready... No. No need to rush things. This small ghost from his past might prove an amusing interlude—but he could afford to wait.

'Well? What did you mean about rats?' she demanded, staring up at him with a slight furrow between her brows.

Richard brought his mind back from the prospect of future diversions, and returned to the immediate present. 'You said something about rats when the photographer failed to take my picture,' he explained.

'Oh.' The lift shuddered to a stop on Deck Three. 'It was just that you dodged away from the camera so quickly that he took my picture instead. I had my mouth open.' She sighed. 'A photo of their mother posing as a fish on the first day of her long-awaited cruise to Europe wasn't exactly the souvenir I'd planned to show off to my children.'

'Children?' Richard frowned. 'Don't tell me you're somebody's mother.' He picked up her cases and strode along the passage to her cabin so fast that she had to run to keep up.

'I suppose you're going to tell me I look too young,' she replied tartly when she managed to catch up with him. 'That line might work on a thirty-five-year-old mother of six, but not on me. I guess I'm not old enough to be flattered.'

'Hmm.' He glanced at her sharply. This funny, surprising young woman didn't strike him as the usual line in harried young mothers. And she had a tongue in her head which she certainly didn't hesitate to use. It amused him in a way. But sooner or later, depending on circumstances, he might have to teach her to curb it. Not an unpleasant task, he decided, his gaze on her tip-tilted nose.

'I'm sorry about the picture,' he said. 'You'd prefer your children to see you as the belle of the boat, I imagine. Not the fish course for dinner.'

Her mouth fell open, then shut quickly as a glimmer of laughter showed in her big pansy eyes. 'I don't really have any children,' she admitted.

'I didn't think you had.'

'I know. You do think I'm too young.' She smiled wryly. 'Or was that just your way of finding out my age?'

'Why should I want to know your age? You look about twenty-two. Which is old enough for me.'

'I'm not available to you, though. And I'm twenty-six.' She sighed. 'Everyone says I look younger.'

He nodded. 'Even better. Tell me, those children you don't happen to have...?'

'No,' she said, looking him directly in the eye. 'I am *not* married. Now, if you don't mind, I'd like to unpack. Thank you very much for your help.'

'My pleasure. Anything else I can do?' He leaned against the doorframe and smiled lazily.

'No, thanks. I can manage just fine now, Mr...?'

'Laslo. Richard Laslo. And you're...?'

'Elfriede Makepeace. Thanks again. I expect I'll see you around.' She shut the door firmly in his face.

Arrogant, thought Elf. Much too sure of himself. She remembered the amused ex-

pression in the ice-green eyes that had narrowed briefly when she told him her name.
He hadn't looked pleased a moment later,
though, when she'd closed the door on him.
Not what he was used to, of course. She
sighed, and wondered if the devastating Mr
Laslo was going to turn out to be a problem.
He must be well aware of his effect on the
opposite sex, and she had to admit that if he
attempted to turn all that Greek god magnetism on her she might not be totally
immune.

She heaved a suitcase on to the bed, re-
calling a slightly crooked mouth and lips that
should have been a little too thin to be sensual.
They weren't, though.

A cream-coloured cocktail dress slid to the
floor in a pile of pale blue tissue, and Elf
picked it up and shoved it into the cupboard.

Funny, there had been something faintly
familiar about Richard Laslo. But she
couldn't have met him before. Even if she
hadn't wasted the last nine months being des-
perately in love with Tony, there was no way
she would have forgotten a hunk like Richard.

She sat down on the edge of the cherry-
flowered bedspread and glanced quickly

around the bright little cabin. It had no port-hole, but it was clean, cheerful and inviting, and she gave herself up to a reverie which for the first time in weeks had nothing whatever to do with Tony.

Richard Laslo, she mused, remembering very long legs and spectacular shoulders en-cased in expensively well cut cloth. 'And all topped off by a lean face with gleaming white teeth and hypnotically sea-green eyes.' She was muttering out loud now, wondering why she felt vaguely resentful that this unlikely vision of glorious manhood was also crowned by a mane of thick fair hair that was a little too long to be fashionable, but which gave him an exotic, almost savage aura. Even his voice was alluring . . .

Elf shook her head and pushed herself off the bed to begin unpacking her clothes in a flurry of determined activity. There was ab-solutely no sense sitting in her cabin mooning over a man she had just met. Not now, on the first day of this holiday she had dreamed of for most of her life—and on which she had already blown far too much of the money she had been saving to start herself up in her own business. Besides, she thought disgustedly, she had wasted quite enough time mooning over Tony lately, and, as she had assured her good friend, Sandra, half the purpose of this extravagant voyage had been to forget about love and romance—and good-looking, two-faced men.

Sandra, she remembered, had laughed at her.

Elf pursed her lips. Her friend could laugh if she liked, but no blond god of a man was going to disrupt *her* holiday. No way.

Shaking her head, she threw half a dozen unnecessary pairs of shoes under the bed, slammed the door behind her, and made her way up to the main deck.

The first scene that met her eyes as she stepped from the lift was a circle of frantic passengers surrounding a small, stocky man whose face was the colour of jaundice. Elf wondered if his colour matched his feelings, and suspected it did, because the entire gesticulating circle seemed to want him to change their dining reservations.

One mother was bleating that her children had not been placed at her table. Another, even more distraught, was complaining that hers *had*. But the loudest voice of all belonged to a statuesque redhead with the voice of a squawking cockatiel.

'This is *terrible*,' she was shrieking. 'I asked for a corner table, with six nice people—by a window—and you've put me in the middle of the room. I would *never* have got such treatment on the *Sunshine Ship*.'

The man with jaundice gave her a sickly smile which made him look like an ailing wax bean, and explained that there were no window tables for six. No corners either.

'Well, it's disgraceful.' The redhead tossed her attractive head and glared at the unfortunate steward. 'Can't you move the tables?'

'I'm afraid not, ma'am. It's impossible to satisfy everyone—but we do try our best.' He looked at her pleadingly, but she only tossed her head again and walked away without answering.

Elf covered her mouth to hide a smile, and as she turned away she caught sight of viking-blond hair waving above spectacular male shoulders. The owner of the shoulders didn't see her, and she withdrew her gaze quickly and hurried towards a flight of curving stairs that led up to a balcony overlooking the ship's forward lounge. When she reached the top, panting a little, she found herself facing a row of shops. Her eyes were drawn immediately to a window display of glitzy evening gowns and sequinned purses. She paused. That slinky little number in yellow silk would just suit her. For that matter, so would everything in the window if she happened to have a few spare thousands.

'Huh,' sniffed a voice in her ear. 'Cheap-looking stuff, isn't it? Poor quality. On the *Sunshine Ship* the shops were much more distinguished.'

The redhead again, of course.

Seen at close quarters, she was gorgeous. She was tall and full-breasted, and her deep blue eyes gazed beguilingly from under the cloud of Titian hair. Pink rose-bud lips were parted in a smile guaranteed to bewitch. Though why she should want to bewitch me I can't imagine, thought Elf wryly. If she'd turned all that eye-power on the dining-room steward, he would probably have moved mountains for her. Tables would have been a cinch.

Conscious that she was staring, Elf smiled hastily. 'I've never sailed on the *Sunshine Ship*,' she explained. 'This is my first cruise.'

'Oh, you poor thing.'

'Why? I'm happy to be here.'

'Poor quality,' sniffed the redhead.

'Not to me, it isn't.' When the other woman wrinkled her nose, Elf added a little defensively, 'My mother grew up in England. I've always wanted to go there. So when I read about this special anniversary crossing it seemed like the perfect opportunity.'

Well, almost perfect, she amended to herself, remembering Richard.

The redhead raised her eyebrows. 'Perfect, did you say? I've sailed on a number of ships, of course, so perhaps I'm a *little* more particular, but I assure you this tub doesn't *compare* to the *Sunshine Ship*. My name's Miranda Bannington, by the way.'

'Elfriede Makepeace,' said Elf, holding out her hand, and wondering if she was supposed to be impressed.

Miranda nodded, and droned on to explain that she was the only daughter of devoted parents who were sending her to England to pick up a rich and titled husband.

Elf was about to say that she didn't think titled husbands hung about on trees in

England, especially rich ones, when she realised that her companion wasn't listening.

'My, oh, my. Look at that dreamboat,' drawled the beauty softly.

Behind a bearded father carrying a child, a long-legged figure in hip-hugging jeans and a T-shirt was mounting the stairs three at a time. Miranda was transfixed, and, to her annoyance, Elf found her own breath catching in her throat.

But he's really *not* handsome, she told herself firmly. His face is too lean and wolf-like.

All the same, she couldn't tear her eyes off it. Nor could Miranda, who had taken a step forward.

The owner of the legs swung round the father and child, then came to a brisk halt as five feet eight inches of undulating redhead swerved in front of him. Dark eyebrows rose coolly above clear green eyes.

'Yes?' Miranda's dreamboat flashed her a cool smile, as his gaze slid over her shoulder and came to rest on Elf with a gleam of speculative recognition.

Colourful, she thought. Irresistible, even to the golden-brown tan. Some people had it all.

'Can you help me?' Miranda was purring at him. 'Silly me, I seem to have lost myself. I'm wondering if *you* can find my cabin?' Her long lashes drooped provocatively, but she lifted them again quickly when the object of the provocation refused to rise to her bait.

'I'd be delighted, naturally, if I hadn't already promised to take Elfriede on a tour of the ship. I think if you just go to the bottom of those stairs, though, you'll find the cruise office directly in front of you. They should be able to help you.'

'Well!' exclaimed Miranda, her blue eyes narrowing nastily. 'That's not very civil of you, Mr...?'

'Laslo. I apologise for any perceived lack of civility, Miss...?'

'Bannington. Miranda.'

'Miss Bannington. But I *did* tell you where to go.'

Elf, who was having trouble with her breathing, made a choking sound. Miranda glanced at her suspiciously, then flounced around to stare at Richard, who was leaning against the balustrade with his bright head thrown back to reveal the strong column of his neck. His gaze met hers with bland and blameless innocence.

'Well, OK,' she muttered, batting her eyelashes. 'I guess you do have to keep your promise. Will I see you later?'

'It's possible,' he said, moving smoothly around Miranda to take Elf's arm. 'Ready, Miss Makepeace?'

As Richard's long fingers curved around her elbow, a quick shock shattered Elf's composure, and just for an instant she found herself leaning against him because she wasn't quite steady on her feet. Then she looked up to see his eyes fixed on her with the anticipatory look of a fox who had just snared a plump chicken dinner, and she straightened quickly.

'I suppose you want to watch the Statue of Liberty fade romantically into the horizon,' he said with an annoyingly patronising smile. 'Everybody does the first time.'

'How do you know it's my first time?'

'By the shine in your lovely brown eyes.'

'Hm. Nice line, Mr Laslo, but not exceptionally original.'

'I'm crushed,' replied Richard, not looking crushed at all. When she tried to pull away, he only tightened his hold and led her along the balcony to the heavy glass doors that led out on to the deck. Once outside, he manoeuvred Elf with practised efficiency through a crowd of milling passengers until he came to a vacant spot by the rail.

When Elf looked round, she found that he was not standing beside her as she'd expected, but leaning nonchalantly against a bulkhead, watching her, with a small, enigmatic smile on his lips. Again she felt that odd stab of recognition—along with a disconcerting sense of abandonment because he was no longer at her side.

He made no move to join her, and, as the ship pulled away from the dock to the accompaniment of laughter and shouted goodbyes, she thought at first that he'd left. Then, when the Statue began to recede into the heat haze, she realised he had moved up beside her. She was uncomfortably aware of the feel of his bare arm against her skin, but he seemed totally absorbed by the view—or what was left of it.

Elf too stared into the distance and, because there was a man beside her, her mind, as it had so often lately, went back to Tony, and then, briefly, to Harry.

Harry had been a medical student. She'd met him at the clinic where she worked, and she had been crazy about him until she discovered that his idea of the ideal 'significant other' was his room-mate—who weighed two hundred and fifty pounds and wore a beard.

After that she had tended to avoid romantic entanglements—until she met Tony in the supermarket, and was sure she'd found true love at last. Newly divorced, he had been standing at the cheese counter looking bewildered as he tried glumly to distinguish Camembert from Brie. Elf had come to his rescue, and fallen instantly for his good looks and natural charm. From then on all her problems had seemed lighter. As long as she had had Tony, the world remained a wonderful place.

As it turned out, she had had him for precisely eight months before she was forced to accept that Tony would never be totally hers. He was still too much in love with his ex-wife, who had left him for a man who raised pigs.

She thought of that last day, of the searing pain that had hit her like a closed fist when the man she loved so completely had admitted, reluctantly and with a certain degree of guilt, that, although he liked Elf well enough, he had no intention of marrying her, and that if she wouldn't sleep with him after all this time—some slim thread of sanity had always held her back from that commitment—then there was no point in continuing the relationship.

Elf had been stunned, disbelieving. She'd thought he was joking at first. But when she said nothing, only stared at him in grief-stricken silence, he had shrugged, kissed her briefly, and left without looking back. Afterwards, she'd collapsed on to her ancient sofa to stare, dry-eyed and empty, at a chip of paint flaking off the wall.

The shock had abated since then, and the crushing hurt, but the sense of aloneness had never really left her. She knew now that the one person she could depend on was herself. It was a lot of the reason she was here on *Supership* now, attempting to put the light back in her life.

Remembering past mistakes, Elf looked up at the man beside her, who had the look of another mistake she could easily be tempted to make. He was leaning over the rail now, staring into the roiling waves, and she noticed that his long legs and seductive backside were attracting more than their share of feminine admiration. She sighed. There was no getting away from it, he *was* astoundingly attractive.

On the other hand, she had left her job and blown half her savings on this dream trip just to get away from memories of a man like him—and to give her battered heart a chance to mend.

'How about that tour of the ship I promised you?' The cool voice, interrupting her reverie, made Elf start.

'You didn't promise,' she told him, coming down to earth with a thump. 'That was just an excuse to get rid of Miranda, wasn't it? Telling tall tales with charming conviction must be one of your many talents, Mr Laslo. And I think she actually believed you.' Elf gave him what she hoped was a suitably dampening frown.

Richard smiled and lifted a dark curl which the soft sea breeze had blown across her forehead. In the clinging summer heat, she shivered suddenly.

'Of course she believed me,' he said.

'Mm.' Elf was thoughtful now. 'Not that I see why you wanted to get rid of her. She *is* gorgeous.'

'Yes, isn't she?' His smile turned reminiscent. 'But I don't like being taken for a fool, and the lady was *not* lost.'

'No, she wasn't. But I doubt if she took you for a fool either. More like——'

'An easy lay?' he suggested drily. 'True. Maybe I am a fool after all. Never mind, there could be—compensations.' His brilliant green eyes raked over her with a suggestion she couldn't misinterpret, and Elf felt her cheeks begin to flame with angry embarrassment.

Self-satisfied, over-confident, much too attractive man, she thought indignantly, pulling her arm away so that their flesh was no longer touching.

Richard smiled, a little malevolently, and took her elbow. When she tried to pull away again, he turned her around, said, 'Let's go,' and, before she could protest, spun her back into the cool relief of the air-conditioned lounge.

'You're very sure of yourself, aren't you?' she taunted.

'Reasonably.' He propelled her ahead of him until they fetched up beside a long, blue-lined swimming-pool that glimmered in the sunlight trapped by a high glass dome. It was surrounded by deckchairs which seemed to be occupied mainly by weary mothers. The pool itself was filled with shrieking, over-excited children.

'Ah. Ankle-biters,' murmured Richard. He stopped abruptly, and glanced pensively from Elf to the pool—and then back again. Observing the direction of his gaze, for one shattering moment she was sure he meant to throw her in.

'Don't you dare,' she cried. 'Just try it and I'll—'

'And you'll what? I hope you're not threatening me, Miss Makepeace. I never refuse a dare.' His grip tightened, and the light of challenge glittered in his eye.

She drew in her breath and tried to break away from him, but his hand seemed to burn through her skin, paralysing her, cutting off the retort that sprang to her lips.

'No, of course I'm not threatening you.' She backed down quickly, deciding discretion was the better part of bravado, and searching her mind for anything that might distract him from the pool. 'If it's all the same to you, I'd just as soon explore the ship on my own. At the moment I could do with a drink.'

'All in good time, Elfriede,' he replied.

Elf felt as if she'd been rebuked for a display of juvenile bad manners. 'Nobody ever calls me Elfriede,' she snapped.

'No,' said Richard. 'They call you Elf.'

'How did you know that?' She gaped at him, and the feeling that there was something she ought to know about him became over-powering.

'I'll tell you one day. If you're good.' She glowered, and he added coolly, 'Behave yourself, and I'll buy you that drink.'

Elf tried to think of a quelling rejoinder, but was distracted when he placed his hand lightly in the small of her back and steered her ahead of him to a small, bright bar upholstered in emerald-green leather.

She was still glowering as he pulled out a chair for her, sat down, and moved a table aside to make room for his endless legs.

Apparently he had no intention of explaining how he knew about her name. Which was his privilege, she supposed, but the mystery was beginning to get under her skin. If mystery it was.

'What are you smiling at?' she asked irritably when she saw his lips curve up. 'We *haven't* met before, have we?'

The smile became coolly cynical, and the muscles around his jawline tightened. Elf was left with a strong feeling that there was more at stake here than he wanted her to know.

'In another life perhaps?' he suggested, with a curious edge to his voice. 'In which I figured as the dreaded villain? It's possible, of course. Do you suppose that might account for your eagerness to extinguish the fuse?'

CHAPTER TWO

ELF stared at Richard across the pale green table which contrasted so attractively with the chairs. 'What fuse?' she demanded.

A steward came to take their order. When he left, Richard leaned back, crossed his legs and replied laconically, 'The fuse that, according to the laws of sexual chemistry, could very well ignite the fire you've been trying so hard to damp down.'

Elf didn't mistake his meaning. And, because he was more than half right, she reacted with an explosiveness that startled her as much as she suspected it surprised—and with any luck annoyed—him.

'You,' she said furiously, 'are a conceited, overbearing, self-centred, arrogant reptile. And if you think every woman you meet is lusting after you, you're an optimist. A deluded optimist.' She started to rise, but Richard caught her wrists and held them so that she couldn't move without creating a scene.

'No, I'm not,' he said evenly. 'I may be overbearing and arrogant, but I don't think I'm particularly conceited. I've encountered too many women whose interest in me has had a lot more to do with my cheque-book than my boyish charm. It's remarkably deflating to the ego, let me tell you. However, as you don't strike me as a lady of the gold-digging persuasion, I hope I have *some* reason for optimism.' He smiled at her in a way that made her squirm. 'What kind of reptile, by the way?'

'Reptile?' Elf stared at him in total blankness until it dawned on her that he was referring to her comprehensive litany of his character flaws. 'A snake, I expect,' she said acidly.

'Hmm.' For a moment the green eyes did look a bit snake-like, and, watching his long body bend towards her, feeling his hands on her arms and his breath brushing over her cheek, Elf found herself battling an excitement that was totally at odds with her, admittedly underdeveloped, sense of self-preservation.

When he released her with a cryptic little smile, she returned to reality and the knowledge that here, in the cocoon-like security of a luxurious bar on this sinfully luxurious ship, not even Richard's virile magnetism could threaten her. For now, at least, she was safe.

'A snake, did you say?' He smoothed a reflective hand over his jaw.

'Well—maybe not a very big one,' she conceded, wishing she didn't sound so breathless. Funny, her indignation seemed to be waning in direct proportion to the movement of the muscles beneath his shirt.

'But poisonous, of course?' he prompted, the expression on his face enigmatic.

Elf fought down an unexpected urge to laugh. 'Only sometimes.'

'You, Miss Makepeace, had better learn to beware of poisonous snakes,' he warned her. 'Especially ones who are only poisonous sometimes.'

'Don't worry, I will,' said Elf shortly.

To her confusion, her answer seemed to amuse him. At least she supposed that was amusement she saw glinting in his unusual green eyes.

'Tell me what you're doing on *Supership*,' he ordered abruptly, and as if he thought he had every right to know.

'Sailing to Europe,' said Elf sweetly. 'What did you think I was doing?'

Richard strummed his fingers on the table. 'Most people fly,' he replied, in a voice that told her he didn't much care for her sarcasm.

'You didn't.'

'No. I'm in no great hurry.'

'But you think I should be?'

'Not necessarily.' His gaze travelled thoughtfully over her face and came to rest on the small hand clenched tightly round the handle of her bag. 'But you appear to be a young lady who is anxious to get where she's going.'

'Not really,' she said, startled out of her irritation and surprised that he should see her that way. 'I want to get to England, of course. But I haven't booked my return yet, so there's no real rush.'

'I see. And you picked *Supership*, for the ultimate ocean experience.'

'Do you mean what's a nice girl like me doing on a boat like this?' Elf hadn't missed the slight undertone of cynicism, and it annoyed her.

'I didn't say anything about nice. Personally I find nice rather dull.'

'That's me,' said Elf, deliberately refusing his bait. 'Dull. *That's* why I chose the ship. It's slower—and it takes time to break out of a rut.' It was taking time to break away from Tony too, but she wasn't about to tell him that.

'What sort of rut?'

She shrugged and replied with an attempt at lightness. 'I've been on my own since I was seventeen. My mother died then, and Dad went completely to pieces. He only survived her by six months.' She paused, puzzled by Richard's sudden frown, and the way his body stiffened in his chair. 'There—there wasn't a lot of money,' she went on when he didn't say anything. 'Just enough for me to take a secretarial course. Eventually I hope to start my own employment agency, so mostly I've been too busy supporting myself and saving pennies to do anything very exciting. That's been my kind of rut.' She sighed. 'And it's quite possible that, if the senior doctor at the clinic where I worked hadn't decided to turn me into his spring project, I'd still be there, instead of blowing my hard-earned cash on a sea voyage.' When Richard lifted an enquiring eyebrow, Elf stared down at the table and explained, 'He offered me a promotion.'

There was silence for a moment, and then Richard asked, 'In return for services rendered? Services of a—personal nature?' His voice was so filled with contempt that Elf blinked.

'Yes. You catch on quickly, Mr Laslo.'

Richard's chiselled lips curved in disdain. 'Didn't you expect me to? No, don't answer that.' He held up his hand. 'In any case, your decision to leave was the right one. I hope you also kicked him in a suitable place.'

This time Elf gave in to that contrary urge to laugh. It was a pleasant surprise to find that Richard felt so strongly on the subject. She had been inclined to take him for the type who would think sexual harassment was a man's God-given right. She was glad she'd been wrong.

'I missed,' she told him regretfully.

'Pity.'

Elf stared at him, curious. He wasn't joking, and she wondered if she'd imagined the depth of repugnance in his voice. And suddenly, as his glacier-deep gaze met her doubtful frown, an odd little chill ran up her spine. There was something about that look... No. She must be crazy. Richard was an attractive, fascinating, and thoroughly aggravating man, not some sinister ogre from a dimly remembered nightmare of the past.

'What do *you* do for a living?' she asked quickly, because it was the first thing she thought of, and she was anxious to take her thoughts off whatever black shadow had surfaced at the back of her mind.

'I'm a jeweller.'

'Oh.'

'That doesn't impress you?' His crooked smile was faintly disbelieving.

'Should it?'

'Not necessarily.'

Elf frowned. Vaguely she thought now that she had heard the name Laslo before in some connection. But she couldn't remember...

'Were you just on holiday in the States, then?' she asked abruptly.

'In a manner of speaking. Combining business with pleasure, you might say. I have some old friends in Los Angeles ——'

'That's where I come from!'

'Amazing. As I was saying, I have old friends there who recently inherited a fortune in antique jewellery. When they asked me to appraise it for them I agreed—and spent a short time appraising the stones, and a long time appraising the scenery.'

'What did you think of it?' asked Elf, who hadn't noted the provocative light in his eye.

'Charming, if a little scantily clad.'

'That's not the kind of scenery I meant.'

'I know.' Richard smiled with a certain malice, and Elf wished she hadn't been so quick to respond. Frowning, she pretended to be absorbed by the loud-voiced couple at the next table who were arguing about which one of them had lost the heartburn pills. When Richard laughed softly, unaccountably she felt her face begin to glow.

'That colour suits you,' he murmured.

The easy sensuality of his smile, and the way his gaze flicked over her as if she were one of the lesser gems up for his personal appraisal, made her want to slap his supercilious face. The blatantly lustful imaginings his look inspired didn't help to cool her temper either.

'I thought,' she said bitingly, 'that you told me you *weren't* under the impression you're God's gift to the single female.'

'Did I say that?' he asked evenly.

'I think so, but——'

'Then I suggest you learn to recognise a compliment when you hear one. And no, I don't think beautiful women were put on earth expressly for my personal convenience. It's a pleasing fantasy, I admit, but not in the least realistic.'

And *she* wasn't beautiful. Was that a compliment too, or was he baiting her again? With this man it was impossible to tell.

'I *didn't* mean——' she began.

'Yes, you did,' Richard cut in crisply. He was silent for a moment and then went on in quite a different voice, 'You're wrong, though. Even if I'd wanted to pursue juvenile fantasies of that nature, I haven't been in any position to indulge them.' The muscles around his jaw tightened. 'Until eleven months ago, that is. And frankly, at that point, I wasn't interested.'

Elf took a quick gulp of her drink. She didn't want to hear about Richard's fantasies—or the lack of them. Nor was she sure she wanted to know what had happened eleven months ago. Looking at him now, she saw a starkness about his features that told her, as words couldn't, that whatever had happened in his past had touched some level of his being that up until now she hadn't thought existed. Perhaps Richard was more than a glib talker with a striking face. The look in his eyes made her flinch.

All the same, she couldn't avoid the knowledge that he confused and disturbed her as Tony never had. When he directed his lethal smile her way, her normal composure deserted her.

Disconcertingly, he was smiling again now, and it wasn't a smile she particularly liked.

'What's so amusing?' she asked, frowning.

'You are,' he drawled. 'You remind me of a porcupine with a bad case of indecision. I promise you, I'm really quite safe.'

Elf's lips curved up in reluctant acknowledgement of his perception. 'I'm sure you are,' she replied, untruthfully.

Richard sat back looking like a hawk which had just selected its next meal.

Forget it, my friend, she thought grimly. I'm no rabbit. And you're not lighting any fuses today.

Almost as if he'd divined her thoughts, Richard swallowed his drink and stood up.

'Ready?' he asked coolly.

'Ready for what?'

His eyes gleamed. 'Not what you think. If you don't mind, I have some business to attend to.'

No, you haven't, thought Elf. You've just had enough of this conversation.

But she stood up too, and a few minutes later, feeling unusually winded, she found herself alone again, leaning limply against the ship's rail.

What on earth was wrong with her? She hardly knew Richard Laslo, but surely he was harmless enough. Why, then, did he seem to have this fatal effect on her heart's normally unfluctuating beat?

Perhaps because he wasn't harmless at all...

Abruptly her thoughts slipped out of gear, and she entertained a brief vision of herself gliding smoothly across a polished dance-floor held tenderly in a pair of strong, masculine arms...

Hold it, Makepeace. You can stop right there. Elf stared down at the dark waves and forced herself to consign the vision to her scrap-pile of abandoned dreams. She knew all too well where that sort of thinking could lead her. In the past it had led to Harry. And then, even more unfortunately, to Tony. Tony, who had not been able to love her...

Surprising herself, and not at all pleasantly, Elf found herself brushing away a tear. She blew her nose vigorously and shook her head. No. She was *not* going to let herself slip back into that old despondency just because a handsome man had paid her some attention and reminded her of what she had lost.

Pushing herself back from the rail, Elf began to walk briskly around the swaying oval deck. The breeze was warm and bracing on her skin, and she sniffed appreciatively at the fresh, salt smell on the sea. This was better. Just what she needed to blow away the trailing cobwebs of past romances—as well as any nonsense about future ones.

She took two more turns round the deck and completed an investigation of several colourfully upholstered bars, two dance-floors, a games-room, a gym, and a plush-looking casino, before retiring to her cabin to dress for dinner.

After a moment's hesitation, she chose a yellow and white striped skirt with matching blouse, and hoped it would do for what was billed as casual first-night attire.

Casual should have read chaotic, she decided a short time later, when she entered the dining-room and saw the crowd of confused and hungry diners swarming through the doors like gourmet bees. To her amusement, though, order was restored within minutes by an efficient young steward who seemed to be doubling as a traffic director. He led Elf to a table near the centre of the room directly beneath a glittering chandelier.

'Good evening.' A slim, white-haired man with a puckish grin rose and bowed to Elf as she took her place at the linen-covered table. 'I'm Jerry Bridger, and this is Elizabeth.' He gestured at a plump woman in her late sixties who was dressed in a dignified black evening gown.

'How nice to have you with us,' said Elizabeth softly. Her smile was sweet, charming, and Elf warmed to her at once. 'I wonder now—is this your first voyage on *Supership*, my dear?'

'Yes, it is,' replied Elf, sitting down. 'Is it your first too?'

'No,' said Jerry with a wicked leer. 'It's our anniversary voyage, isn't it, Elizabeth? We met at this table five years ago. She lives in Cornwall and I live in Florida, but we meet on the high seas once a year.' He pursed his small mouth primly. 'Our children think we're with a respectable group of touring seniors——'

'Jerry,' began Elizabeth repressively.

'But actually we're living in sin,' he finished, with an elfin smile at his companion, who tried not to smile back and failed.

'Very sensible,' drawled a familiar voice over Elf's head. 'Don't you agree, Miss Makepeace?'

'I—er—don't...' Elf stuttered, as long fingers brushed casually against her neck, and a tall figure in pale grey linen eased itself on to the chair next to hers.

'Don't what? Live in sin? I'm glad to hear it.'

Jerry chuckled, and Richard introduced himself. 'Richard Laslo. I imagine you've already met Elfriede Makepeace.'

'Who?' asked Jerry and Elizabeth in unison.

'Me. And my name's Elf,' she said firmly.

'That's a relief.' Jerry laughed. 'Are you two travelling together?'

'Alas, no.' Richard pulled a mournful face at Elf, who found herself wanting to laugh but managed not to.

When two more people arrived at the table she decided there wasn't much to laugh about after all. One was a very fat young man with spectacles.

The other was Miranda.

'Good evening, Miss Bannington.' Richard turned immediately to the newcomer, and Elf saw the corner of his lip lift slightly as his gaze fell on the deep-dish cleavage of her clinging jade-green dress.

'Good evening, Mr Laslo.' As the waiter came up to take their orders, Miranda batted long, beautifully mascaraed eyelashes and toyed daintily with the stem of her wine glass. It was apparent that her discontent with the dining arrangements had undergone a radical reversal.

The woman's just like candyfloss, thought Elf with unusual bitterness. All pink sugar and no substance.

She studied the super-abundance of the menu and at once felt even more out of sorts.

Here was every exotic food she'd ever heard of, and she had to be sitting with a man as exotic as the food, along with a gloriously slim charmer who could probably eat everything from horses to suet pudding without it showing.

'Well, I don't care,' she muttered under her breath. 'I'm going to eat what I like, even if I do roll off the ship looking like a butterball turkey.'

'Did you say something?' asked Richard.

'No,' replied Elf curtly. She was uncomfortably conscious of his nearness, and resentful that, with at least a hundred other tables in the room, he had chanced to be seated at this one.

'I could have sworn you did,' he murmured.

Elf ignored him, and concentrated on the menu. In the end she ordered a large plate of pasta with clam sauce. To her surprise, when it arrived, she saw Miranda eyeing her plate with envy while she herself tucked into a spinach salad.

So the beauty had to watch her weight after all. Elf began to feel better.

Conversation swirled around her, and the fat man, who had been morosely silent before the food arrived, volunteered, between mouthfuls, that he was Charles P. Waterbush from Virginia, after which he returned with total concentration to his food.

Richard, Elf noticed, managed to eat a substantial meal and at the same time maintain casual conversation with those around him. He had a talent for putting everyone except herself at ease. She noted his skill with a flick of irritation that was beginning to feel almost familiar.

'I suppose you young ladies will be dancing the night away beneath the moon,' said Jerry as soon as the coffee came. 'Unlike us tired old fogies.'

Elf, catching Richard's eye on her, shook her head quickly. 'Oh, no. I'm a fogey myself. I'll be going to bed.'

Richard picked up his cup and eyed her reflectively over its brim. 'An excellent idea.'

Elf swallowed the last of her coffee, choked, and jumped quickly to her feet. 'Excuse me,' she mumbled. 'I hope you don't mind, but I'm a little tired tonight. It's been a long day.'

'No question about it, then,' said Richard with a smile so bland that she wanted to punch him on his arrogant nose. 'Bed's the perfect place for you.'

'Oh, cut it out,' Elf snapped, stepping backwards and knocking over her chair.

Richard picked it up without comment. But as Elf turned away she caught an aggravating glimpse of his face. It was lit with a devilish mirth that sent her blood-pressure soaring.

Quivering with annoyance, she marched out of the dining-room with her head high and her bag swinging wildly from her shoulder. But when she reached the double doors of the entranceway she paused.

She might, for want of a better story, have told Richard she was going to bed. But she wasn't. Not on her first night at sea.

Laughing passengers jostled past her. One of them, a skinny girl with pink hair, bumped her elbow, and on an impulse Elf decided to follow her. She had to go somewhere before Richard finished his coffee and left the dining-room to find her standing in everyone's way like a misplaced statue. She'd had enough of Richard Laslo for one night.

It turned out that the pink-haired girl was making for the ship's nightclub, an intimate, low-ceilinged room with a blue and white checkerboard floor.

Elf gazed at the dreamy-eyed couples gathering under the shaded lights to dance, and, as the band began to warm up, she came to the reluctant conclusion that without a partner this wasn't where she wanted to be. But the room was dimly lit, she could lose herself in the crowd and, if she was lucky, the bar steward might be persuaded to serve her a shamefully fattening pink soda.

He did, although Elf noticed he kept glancing at her sideways as if he regarded patrons who drank pink sodas as being from another planet.

She looked around for a seat, but they were all taken, so she collected her glass and propped herself up against the bar.

'Well, well, well,' murmured an unmistakable voice into her ear. 'Did you find you couldn't sleep after all? I wonder now—what could possibly have kept you awake?'

Elf jumped, and the best part of her pink soda shot out to land in a foamy pink stream across the counter.

'Rats,' she muttered.

'Quite so,' said the voice agreeably. 'Here, let me.' Tapered masculine fingers reached for a sponge that was lying on the counter, and a capable hand curled around her wrist. When Richard began to mop her up with a hard thoroughness that reminded her of the brisk ministrations of her kindergarten teacher, Elf seized the sponge from his hands and continued the job herself.

Richard's eyes narrowed. 'You think maybe I make a hobby of breaking fingers?'

Elf flinched. He wasn't teasing her, he was issuing a rebuke. Presumably women didn't usually reject his assistance. It particularly annoyed her that his touch had caused a flick of desire to snake its way up through her body.

'No,' she replied levelly. 'I think maybe I'm quite capable of cleaning up my own messes. What's left of them.' She added that because a blank-faced steward was busy wiping the sticky evidence from the counter. 'Besides which, I was enjoying my own company, thank you.'

Richard shrugged. 'In that case, far be it from me to deprive you of such riveting society.'

He turned away, and Elf, furiously and un-characteristically, picked up the sponge again and hurled it at his elegantly departing back.

'Patronising bastard,' she muttered.

The back stopped departing at once and reversed direction. Richard stepped over the sponge as if it weren't there and loomed above her. He was standing so close now that their chests were almost touching.

'You shouldn't have done that,' he said softly.

Elf stared into his hard green eyes and ex-perienced an unexpected curl of excitement which she knew she wasn't meant to be feeling. He looked sexy and overpowering, and she found herself rising to a challenge that was no less explicit because it wasn't spoken.

'No.' She decided to deflect the challenge. 'I shouldn't. It was childish of me.'

There. That should take the wind from his sails. She picked up the sponge and placed it on the counter, smiling sheepishly at the blank-faced steward, who removed it without moving a muscle of his face.

'Yes,' agreed Richard. 'It was. Childish and not very wise.'

She frowned. 'What do you mean?'

'Just that I don't accept impertinence from children, and I'm not about to accept it from you.'

Elf gasped. 'Well, of all the arrogant——'

Her words were cut off as he put his hands on her hips and pulled her up against him. To her fury, her body reacted at once to the feel of his hard frame through her clinging skirt. She tried to pull away, but he wouldn't let her, and as he slid his firm hands over her lower back she knew with devastating certainty that he meant to kiss her.

Unbidden, that maddening flick of desire came again, and wound up warm and pulsing in her stomach. She damped it down ruthlessly.

'Don't you dare——' she began.

Richard ignored her. His gaze was fixed on her face, and in the sea-green depths of his eyes she saw a reflection of something she didn't understand. Anger, certainly, and a determination to exact a penalty for the flying sponge. But there was also a kind of frustration, a reluctance to do what she knew he intended to do.

The realisation galvanised her into a futile attempt to squirm her way out of his embrace. It proved the wrong thing to do, because he tightened his grip.

The music slowed, became softer, insinuating its way into her consciousness like smoke. Then the tempo changed again, and the band began to play a throbbing, erotic melody. A spotlight flickered over her face. Disorientated, dizzy with unwanted longing, Elf closed her eyes.

An arm jostled her elbow and immediately Richard lowered his mouth over hers.

His kiss was hard, purposeful, without tenderness, and yet she was horrified to find herself fighting not to respond. In the end she lost the battle, and, as a drugging need subdued her resistance and turned her limbs heavy with desire, she parted her lips willingly and surrendered to the pleasure of his probing tongue.

But as she clung to him, oblivious of time or of place, Richard lifted his head and held her briskly away.

'Penalty exacted and quite nicely paid,' he said, so dismissively that at once she was reminded of Tony. A great emptiness seemed to gape in front of her then, before, fortunately, pride and indignation took over.

'How dare you?' she demanded.

Before he could answer, her back collided with something soft, which turned out to be the expansive bosom of a mildly outraged matron in flowered chiffon.

'Really,' muttered the matron. 'Disgraceful...'

When Richard, with a resigned lift of his eyebrows, attempted to move Elf out of the way, she scowled at him and dodged behind the counter.

The steward, looking blanker than ever, politely asked her to move, and Elf felt an unexpected need to blow her nose. She shuffled to the very end of the bar and began to grope through her handbag for a tissue.

Finally, when she had pulled out three lipsticks, a collection of pennies, a broken comb, two scrunched-up balls of silver paper and three false fingernails which she had once thought might make her life easier, she became aware that Richard was eyeing the collection with a look that betrayed masculine amazement at the frivolous priorities of women.

Tightening her lips, and hoping that in the dim lighting of the nightclub he couldn't see the colour of her face, Elf shoved the nails to the bottom of the bag and snapped it shut.

'Did you find what you were looking for?' asked Richard.

He knew she hadn't. And he was an over-bearing, overpowering man who happened to be blessed with the body of a blond god and the sexual magnetism of a James Bond. Lucky for him, she thought viciously. But, just because she had foolishly succumbed for a moment, there was no reason why she should put up with any more of his games. She was *not* going to go to pieces just because one devastating but thoroughly irritating man had kissed her. It wasn't as if she were sweet sixteen any more. And she had been kissed very thoroughly by Tony.

Yes, but never quite like tonight.

She pushed the thought away and blew her nose on a napkin from the dispenser. 'No,' she said to him. 'I didn't find it, and, if you don't mind, I'm very tired—particularly of men who think they can have anything they want just because they're handsome and male. I'm going to bed.'

'I said that was the best place for you,' murmured Richard, sliding his hands into his pockets and lounging back against the counter with a mocking little smile on his lips. '"There was an old woman who lived in a shoe..."'

Elf blinked. 'What?' she asked stupidly.

'"Who had so many children, she didn't know what to do".'

Elf began to get his drift. '"She gave them some broth without any bread..."'

'"And whipped them all soundly and sent them to bed",' he finished, brushing a speck of dust off his sleeve. 'They had primitive ideas about child-rearing in those days, didn't they? Though at times like this I can certainly see the advantages.'

Elf glared at him. 'I am not a child, if that's what you're trying to imply.'

'I know. I'd noticed.'

Quite suddenly, something about his aquiline features disturbed her, and she felt a sharp stab of a fear she couldn't, for the life of her, understand. She licked her lips and took a quick step backwards.

'What are you afraid of, Elf?' His green gaze was very hard and perceptive.

Fear faded, was replaced by irritation. 'Certainly not of you,' she snapped. 'Goodnight, Mr Laslo.' Without waiting for him to answer, she spun around and marched out of the room, half expecting that Richard would try to stop her. But he didn't.

When she reached her cabin, she banged the door shut behind her and flung herself down on the bed. The ship heaved and groaned in sympathy beneath her, and, as she stared up at the ceiling, gradually her irritation subsided. So did any residue of that sudden, irrational dread.

She sat up, patting vaguely at a smear of lipstick on the pillow.

There was no point in continuing a feud with Richard. Nor was there any sense in allowing herself to be drawn into his admittedly magnetic orbit. That kiss had been intoxicating, but she had only met him today, he was probably just a man on the make, and she was in no mood for that sort of entanglement. Not now when her heart was still raw. Besides, there was something else. Some faint worm of memory... She shook her head. It couldn't be important, and she wasn't normally afraid of shadows. Shadows weren't real. Any more than those false fingernails had been. Remembering, she reached for her bag, intending to throw them away.

It wasn't there.

Rats. She must have left it sitting on the bar.

Wearily Elf pulled herself on to her feet. Then she straightened her crumpled skirt before taking the lift back to the nightclub she had so recently left.

The band was grinding out a thundering beat, and as soon as Elf crossed the threshold she caught sight of Richard's formidable figure moving sinuously across her vision beneath a spotlight.

He was holding Miranda in his arms.

The redhead's hands were clasped behind his neck, and her bountiful breasts were pressed against his chest. He held her loosely, his hands just touching her hips, and he was staring over her shoulder at the band. But when Miranda whispered something into his ear he lowered his head a little and whispered back.

Elf brushed a hand over her eyes and took a quick step into the shadows, surprised to find that she didn't much like what she was seeing. She watched as Richard's lips moved in answer to some remark of Miranda's, then she turned away, retrieved her bag from the bar steward, who handed it to her without comment, and took the lift back to Deck Three.

From the other side of the dance-floor Richard watched her go, and he smiled distantly as Miranda prattled on about what a wonderful dancer he was and how attracted she was to tall men. The feel of her curves against his body was quite stimulating, he thought dispassionately. It had been almost twelve months since Felicity, and there wasn't much doubt about what he was being offered at this moment... He smiled cynically and glanced down at the bright hair waving down his partner's slender neck.

The beauty wriggled voluptuously in his arms.

A few dedicated joggers were pounding their way round the deck when Elf wandered outside the next morning after breakfasting on croissants in her cabin. In a quiet corner she caught sight of Jerry Bridger and a small group of yoga enthusiasts stoically standing on their heads. Otherwise the deck was deserted. The hot sun was behind them now, and the ship was enveloped in heavy Atlantic clouds.

Elf sniffed the misty air and went to stand by the rail. Huge, foam-flecked rollers heaved below her, and she wondered why on this, her first morning at sea, she felt curiously listless and alone. Funny, she had thought she was used to loneliness by now. Surely she wasn't going to be seasick?

Her musings were interrupted abruptly by three raucous blasts from the ship's siren.

'Rats,' she muttered, as the ringing in her ears faded, and Jerry and his little company bounded on to their feet. 'Lifeboat drill.' She had forgotten all about it.

She hurried down to her cabin, and some minutes later arrived, breathless and gasping, among her fellow passengers on the boat deck. It was as she was leaning against a bulkhead with her eyes closed that she felt someone tap her on the shoulder.

'Your lifejacket is on backwards,' said a man's voice.

She turned to find herself staring into Richard's eyes. They were darker this morning, bruised-looking, no longer a bright green enigma. Perhaps he hadn't slept any better than she had. If he'd slept at all.

'Oh, it's you,' she said, with carefully assumed indifference. 'Of course it's not on backwards.' She stole a quick look at her bulky orange figure. 'Is it?'

'I wouldn't have said it was if it wasn't. Here, you do it this way.' Taking her by the shoulders, Richard expertly reversed the jacket, wrapped the tapes behind her and then brought them round to the front. Elf, feeling a little dazed, decided it was just as well the bulk of the jacket precluded more intimate contact, because when his hands brushed briefly over her breasts she experienced a jolt of pure bodily need that was almost enough to knock her off her feet.

She swallowed, and stepped back hastily.

'You're gasping like a beached bloater,' Richard observed conversationally. 'What's the matter?'

'Nothing. I forgot about the drill and I've been running.'

'I see.' His eyes, weary but none the less compelling, appraised her with undisguised amusement. 'No, on second thoughts, not a bloater. A lobster. As I've mentioned before, that colour suits you.'

'I can't help my complexion,' snapped Elf, who was breathless for more reasons than one, and not in any mood for clever banter. 'And I can't help it if I remind you of last night's seafood.'

Richard's lips quirked and he turned away from her to gaze pensively up at the clouds. 'I like seafood,' he remarked, pushing his hands into his pockets. 'Very appetising.'

Elf glared at him, and, when he glanced down and saw her expression, his features sobered. 'Don't look at me like that,' he ordered. 'I don't like it.'

She opened her mouth to tell him that she didn't give a damn what he liked, but, before she could get the words out, his lips had parted in a maddeningly seductive smile.

Elf gulped, started to say something, then realised he wasn't looking at her any more. Turning, she followed the direction of his eyes, and saw that Miranda had just sauntered on to the deck.

She frowned, wondering how the red-headed bombshell managed to look gorgeous even when she was swathed in orange rubber.

Her carefully made-up eyes showed no sign at all of fatigue.

'Hello, Richard,' she shrilled, sounding like a cockatiel again.

'Good morning, Miranda. No problems with your lifejacket, I see.'

Miranda fluttered her eyelashes. 'As a matter of fact my steward helped me out. He was very kind.'

I'll bet, thought Elf sourly, as the other woman lifted a languid arm to sweep her auburn locks back from her neck.

'No doubt,' said Richard indifferently. 'That's his job.'

Elf glanced at him, confused and obscurely relieved. That didn't sound like the remark of a man who had spent the night making love to Miranda...

The officer in charge of the drill appeared then, to give his speech about emergency procedures. The passengers listened politely, shivering in the chill morning air, and as soon as he was finished most of them shuffled back inside. Like a bunch of homing beach balls heading for warmth, thought Elf wryly. She supposed she looked a lot like a beach ball herself.

Miranda shivered gracefully. 'Would you like to come down to my cabin for a while, Richard? Just to warm up,' she added with a coquettish smirk.

'What? After poached eggs for breakfast?' Richard raised a disbelieving eyebrow.

Miranda's mouth fell open. 'Well, really!' she exclaimed. 'What an odd thing to say.'

'Poached eggs? Odd? I don't see why.'

'Well, really.' The beauty frowned at him, puzzled and quite out of her depth. When he responded to the frown with a smile of implacable charm, she turned on her heel to hurry after a large male beach ball wearing Gucci shoes and an expensive-looking watch.

Elf and Richard were left alone in the greyness. She looked away from him, and buried her face in her hands.

'What's the matter?' he demanded impatiently of her shaking shoulders.

'You are,' she mumbled through her fingers. 'Poached eggs...'

'Mmm,' he murmured, placing a hand on her arm. 'I'm fond of eggs.' When her body continued to shake, he added peremptorily, 'Stop it, Makepeace. You're giggling like a silly schoolgirl. I want to talk to you.'

'What about?' asked Elf, still laughing as Richard turned her around to steer her back into the lounge.

He didn't answer until they had dropped their lifejackets on to the carpet and settled into two comfortable armchairs set beside the window.

'About us,' he replied then, smiling lazily and as if it were the most obvious answer in the world.

Elf frowned. 'What about us?'

Richard rested an ankle on his knee, flexed his shoulders and contemplated the tip of his shoe. When he looked up he said, 'Don't you know? I thought you were quicker on the uptake.'

'Oh. I'm beginning to see.' Elf dug her fingers into the arm of her chair. 'A little premature, aren't you?'

'Premature?' He shrugged. 'I don't think so.'

'Don't you?' she said through her teeth. 'In that case perhaps I should remind you that my last boss offered me a promotion for what you're about to suggest. What do *you* have to offer?'

CHAPTER THREE

THERE was a long, dangerous pause during which Richard stared at her as if she were some grub he'd found in his lettuce. 'And what,' he enquired when he decided to end it, 'do you mean by that questionable remark?'

Elf forced herself to sit straight, not to betray that the look, and the way he was curling his fingers into fists, made her feel horribly ill at ease.

'What do you think?' she gibed.

The line of his mouth hardened. 'I think you've just made the kind of suggestion I'd have expected from some gold-digging popsie. Not from you.'

Elf felt as if she'd been hit in the face. Had she totally misread Richard's intentions then? He had said he wanted to talk about 'us'. But there wasn't any 'us'. They were just two people who had recently met, so naturally she had thought he was suggesting a convenient and very common arrangement by which one party provided certain services, and the other paid for them with job promotions, jewellery and expensive clothing. And she'd been hurt and angry because she hadn't expected that of him. He had seemed so disgusted when she told him about her boss's unwanted attentions...

Oh, lord. She put her hand up to her mouth. Was it possible that he felt insulted too?

She searched for words to explain. A way to find out. 'I—you—I thought you were suggesting—well, something that's quite different from marriage.' She swallowed. 'Weren't you?'

Briefly, Richard stopped looking coldly contemptuous and looked stunned. Then he shrugged and said in a voice that held no hint of emotion, 'Wasn't I what? Suggesting marriage?'

Elf gaped at him. '*Marriage*?' she exclaimed, as if she'd never heard the word before.

'Yes. You know. As in wedding bells, floral arrangements, gold rings and ˙ arguments about who should be sent an invitation.'

For a moment Elf was struck dumb. His tone was careless, deliberately bored, but there was a tension in the strong angle of his jaw and the long fingers strumming against his thigh that confused her utterly. Was he serious? Was he making some kind of convoluted proposal? Swallowing again, she decided the only way to find out was to ask.

'Are you asking me to marry you?' She spoke clearly, looking straight ahead and trying not to let her eyes be drawn to the movement of muscles beneath his dark blue T-shirt.

Richard shrugged himself back in his chair, stretched his legs and looked her over from top to toe as if he was trying to decide if she met his requirements.

'Why not?' he said finally. 'Is that what you want?'

This time she found her voice at once. 'What? No, it most certainly isn't. Why on earth should I want to marry *you*? I hardly know you ——'

'And what you do know, you don't much like? Well, we'll just have to change that, won't we?' He smiled, a feral sort of smile that made her leap up as if she'd been scalded. She'd had as much of this unlikely conversation as she could take.

With lightning speed Richard leaned forward and seized her hands.

'Sit still. I want to talk to you, not assault you in full view of several hundred fellow passengers. Including Charles P. Waterbush,' he added, as that well padded gentleman plodded past munching morosely on a bar of milk chocolate.

Elf didn't respond. Instead she perched on the edge of her seat and gazed at him as if she doubted his sanity. Which, come to think of it, she did.

'You're right,' he said. 'You don't know me. But, if you ask the right questions, I may answer.'

'Questions?' Elf was taken aback. 'About what?'

He shrugged. 'Me, I suppose. Although I had hoped I was a whom and not a what.'

'Debatable,' she replied with icy sweetness.

'Watch it, Makepeace, or —— '

'Or *what*?' snapped Elf, belatedly pulling her hands away. She felt as if she were losing control of her senses—and she didn't like it.

Richard smiled obliquely. 'Or I may withdraw my offer. No, don't stab me with those daggers from your pansy-flower eyes,' he added, when he saw Elf's generous mouth flatten into a pancake. 'Just try to pretend I'm human, and ask away.'

Elf took a deep breath. She wanted to get up and leave this impossible man to his own devices, but there was something about the way he was looking at her that made her hesitate. If she wasn't altogether mistaken, he *expected* her to retreat.

Well, she wasn't going to.

'All right. What about you?' she challenged. 'Are you—er——?'

'No,' he said caustically. 'I'm not spoken for.'

'Oh! Of all the—I wasn't going to—I didn't imagine...' She stopped, started again. 'I hadn't imagined you were,' she finished lamely.

She hadn't either. It didn't fit in with his talk of marriage, although that, of course, had been a game. The kind of game two could play at.

'OK,' she said lightly. 'So you're available. In that case, I might take you up on your offer.'

Richard didn't look at all discomposed. 'Might you?' he said. 'And on what does your acceptance depend?'

Elf pretended to consider. 'Well,' she murmured, 'I suppose it could depend on the number of ex-wives you have lurking in the background. All pining their hearts out for you, of course.'

To her surprise, Richard didn't reply in the same vein, and when she tried to meet his eyes she discovered that he was staring right through her. It was almost as if she weren't there. Puzzled, she repeated the question, and he came back from wherever he had been, lifted his head and said quietly, 'Not a string, no. Just one. And I assure you she's in no position to pine. For me, or for anyone else.'

'Oh.' Elf wondered why her stomach felt as if it had just dropped six inches. She gave a small sigh, saw Richard's eyebrows lift a fraction, and wished her thoughts weren't always so transparent. 'You're divorced, then,' she said, somehow not at all surprised.

'No. My wife died eleven months ago. If she'd lived, tomorrow would have been our tenth anniversary.'

'Oh. Oh, Richard, I *am* sorry. I wouldn't have asked...' Elf stared at him in consternation, as all her preconceptions dropped away. 'Did you ——? Yes, of course you did.'

'Did I what?'

She twisted her fingers in her lap. 'I was going to ask if you loved her very much, but of course ——'

'Love?' he interrupted with a bleak derision that made her squirm. 'You subscribe to that fantasy, do you?' When he saw Elf staring at him, he brushed a hand over his eyes and finished wearily, 'I miss her, if that's what you mean. Much more than I ever expected.'

'Oh.' Elf didn't quite know what to say to that. 'Weren't you happy?' she asked finally, not sure it was any of her business, but feeling some comment was required.

Richard removed a piece of fluff from his trousers. 'Oh, Felicity and I were happy enough,' he said. 'I had my work, she had her horses.'

'Work and horses? That's an odd definition of married bliss.'

'I didn't say anything about bliss.' His tone was curt. 'We had a good working relationship and we were friends. We'd known each other since we were children. Everyone expected us to marry.'

'People don't always do what's expected of them.' Elf didn't add, Especially you, I think. But she thought it.

'Very true. But in this case I expected it of myself.'

Elf frowned. She didn't understand this. Richard had lost a wife he had known most of his life, and been content with—and yet he was acting as if he'd mislaid a useful sporting dog instead of a beloved wife and friend. Was he, perhaps, concealing a hurt far deeper than he was willing to admit? Or was guilt behind that air of indifference?

'What—what happened to Felicity?' she asked. Perhaps he wanted to talk, although she didn't think he was the sort of man who normally wore his heart on his sleeve.

'She fell off a horse. Exactly the end she would have chosen.'

'Oh, how...' Elf had been about to say, How awful, but Richard looked so forbidding now that the words died on her lips.

'Yes, it was a shock,' he said crisply. 'But it was quick.'

She nodded. 'Truly, I am sorry.' There didn't seem much else to say.

'I know you are.' Richard gave her a steady look that she found surprisingly disconcerting. 'You're that sort of woman.'

'You don't know what sort of woman I am.'

'I think I do. You're as prickly and independent as a damned porcupine, but you're lonely too, and your prickles conceal a dangerously soft heart. You can't stand to see anything hurt, can you, including me?' His lip curled up in what Elf took for disparagement. 'But you're resilient, I'll give you that, and maybe more adventurous than you know.'

'Thanks for the analysis,' said Elf drily. She felt a little hurt, but wondered if he was right about her being adventurous. It *had* taken a certain amount of recklessness to blow so much of her savings on this trip. Maybe this unusual interpretation of her character had been behind his careless proposition. He hadn't been serious about marriage, of course, but he was a man—with a man's appetites. Maybe he thought she was hungry too. Unconsciously, she moistened her lips. If he thought that, he could just think again. *He* wasn't the sort of adventure she needed. After Tony she was wary of ex-wives. Dead ones she wouldn't even consider.

When she glanced at Richard again she saw that he was studying her as if he were a military tactician looking for a weak point in enemy defences. And he didn't look tired any more. In fact he looked tanned, confident and impossibly sexy.

She turned away, shaken by conflicting emotions she didn't understand.

At once she felt his fingers beneath her chin, as her head was tilted up to face him.

She stiffened.

'There's really no need to be afraid of me,' he said softly, sensing her tension. 'I don't think you're afraid of much else.' He stroked his thumb down her neck, and she trembled, wanting to pull away, yet mesmerised by the hypnotic green of his eyes.

'You're a tough little lady, aren't you?' he murmured, half to himself. 'But tender in all the right places.'

'Don't,' said Elf, her heart fluttering crazily. 'Don't, Richard.'

'Don't what?' His hand was cradling the back of her head now, pushing through the curls on her neck.

'Don't—don't . . .'

'Don't kiss you?' His voice was smooth, silky and warm. 'Elf, have you any idea how easily you could drive a sane man crazy?'

And did he have any idea that he *was* driving a sane woman crazy?

'I—I . . .' She couldn't get the words out, because his lips were hovering just above hers, and the cool male scent of him was in her nostrils. Then he was kissing her, gently at first, then harder as his tongue slid in between her teeth.

Elf raised her hands to clasp them on his shoulders, shaken by a hunger she had never expected to know, never believed existed outside the pages of lurid novels. She made a small sound as Richard locked his arms around her and drew her on to her feet. Then they were standing, so close that she could feel every hard, intoxicating angle of his body. His thumb began to revolve slowly at the base of her spine, and his lips tasted of warm earth and rich, creamy coffee. She clung to them with a need that frightened her a little. Even with Tony, she had never known desire like this.

It was Richard who finally pulled away. There were minute drops of moisture on his forehead.

'Well, Makepeace,' he drawled, flicking a curl out of her eyes. 'That got a bit out of hand, didn't it?'

Elf nodded, still unable to speak, and saw that their corner of the lounge wasn't as private as she'd thought. People were watching them surreptitiously, some wearing nostalgic smiles, others frowning. She flushed uncomfortably. But if Richard was aware of the onlookers he didn't care about them. His seductive mouth was tilted at an arrogant angle, and his eyes—his eyes were as cool as green glass.

She took a step backwards, and he pulled a handkerchief from his pocket and ran it across his forehead.

'How about a swim?' he suggested. 'Apart from a quick trip to my cabin, which I rather suspect you'll decline, it's the only alternative I can think of to a cold shower. Coming?'

Elf gaped at him. 'For a shower or a swim?' she asked, without pausing to think. When she saw his eyebrows lift, she added quickly, 'You're right about my declining.'

Richard's lips twitched. 'Is there a shower in *your* cabin?' he asked.

Elf's mouth fell open in consternation. 'No,' she gasped. 'I mean, yes, but...'

'Ah. In that case I vote for a shower.'

'Think again. You don't *have* a vote, Richard Laslo.'

'I thought you'd say that.' Richard shrugged. 'Never mind, I'm a patient man, and I generally get what I want in the end. Meet me by the pool in ten minutes.' He turned his back, confident that she would do as she was told.

Elf watched him cross the lounge, oblivious to the heads turning as he passed, and she vowed not to go anywhere near the pool. Apart from the fact that she resented his dictatorial manner, she was unwilling to admit to this athletic-looking Adonis that swimming, to her, meant no more than a quick splash in the shallows.

On the other hand, if she didn't go, it would be a terrible waste of her new yellow bikini...

Five minutes later she was pulling the bikini from underneath a pile of lacy underwear and thinking vaguely that it was too bad she had never learned to swim. But she'd been nervous around water since childhood. And anyway, as Tony had once unkindly informed her, she looked like a double-jointed frog in the water. Not that Tony had seen her in the yellow bikini...

She put it on and studied her figure in the mirror, turning from side to side to detect any hitherto unsuspected bulges. Patting her stomach, she decided that, if she could manage to stay off desserts for the rest of the voyage, her body might do passably well.

And who do you think you're trying to impress? she asked herself in disgust, as she draped a big white towel over her shoulders and tossed her short curls at her reflection. She sighed. There wasn't much point in replying to that question, because the answer was maddeningly obvious.

And that kiss should never have happened.

Only it had, and her world seemed to have slipped off its axis.

Elf was still feeling confused and irritated with herself when she arrived beside the pool a short while later. For one thing, she half regretted coming. Richard might be used to getting what he wanted, but *she* wasn't used to being bossed around. Apart from which, every sane instinct was screaming at her that he would be a disastrous man to get involved with. Even if she hadn't sworn off men on a temporary basis, there was something about this particular man, who would have celebrated ten years of marriage tomorrow, that made her apprehensive...

Elf glanced across the blue-green water, wondering if there was still time to retreat. Then she clutched her towel a little more closely as her eyes fell not on the man who had so recently kissed her, but on the golden and gorgeous vision of Miranda in a cream bikini. She looked like a Technicolor Aphrodite reclining on a padded deckchair, with her arms behind her head and her thick hair spread fetchingly across the cushions. The eyes of every man—and most of the women—on deck were fixed on her in either hope or envy.

Elf sighed quietly. She didn't feel envy exactly, but a sort of wistful regret. The redhead was undeniably lovely—and long legs and a willowy body had always been her own ideal of feminine beauty—perhaps, as Harry had once said quite kindly, because she could never hope to possess them herself.

'Star-gazing?' enquired a voice.

'I suppose I am. So is everyone else,' replied Elf flatly.

Richard moved up beside her, and she saw that he was wearing enticingly brief white bathing shorts. The sight of his nearly naked body, bronzed, lean, and rippling with animal health and vitality, made her choke back a gasp.

She wanted to reach out and touch him. But she didn't because, quite casually, he took her arm—and the athletic leanness of his body and the taut strength of his bare arms and thighs distracted her so badly that she found herself unable to speak. He was standing so close to her that she was sure that if she moved just a fraction her own body would fit perfectly into his...

Elf gulped, mumbled something unintelligible, and ground to a halt like a car which had run out of gas.

Richard's gaze moved slowly over her small figure in the neat bikini—which suddenly began to seem like a mistake. He made no effort to move away, and for a moment Elf thought she would drown in the ocean-green depths of his eyes.

She took a step backwards, forcing herself to remember her surroundings. Richard, continuing to hold her arm as if he had right of possession, followed her to the edge of the pool. She was just thinking that no man had any business to look so breathtakingly desirable, when a small girl slammed into them from behind. She heard Richard's seductive laugh ring out as the three of them splashed into the water in a confusion of white spray and limbs.

The child swam away giggling, and Elf, gasping and spluttering, made a frantic grab for the edge.

I must look like a new-born whale, she thought gloomily, her momentary alarm subsiding as her hand connected with the rail. Now not even the yellow bikini could hide her aquatic ineptitude from the world. And the world *does not* mean Richard, she insisted to herself without conviction, as she watched him swim towards her with long-limbed, easy strokes.

She saw the drops glistening on his golden body and the fair hair plastered to his head.

Overcome, she drew in her breath, telling herself she was thankful that they were surrounded by other swimmers. Because if they hadn't been . . .

She suppressed the thought ruthlessly.

'You'll have to let go of that rail sooner or later,' he murmured, his strong hands circling her waist beneath the water.

Elf pulled back. 'Didn't I tell you I can't swim?' she said quickly.

'Can't swim? In all these years . . . ?' Richard's mouth curled up in what she supposed was derision. 'Don't be ridiculous, of course you can.' When she continued to cling obstinately to the rail, he said impatiently, 'Come on, Makepeace. I'll teach you.' Taking his hands from her waist, he circled an arm underneath her breasts. She felt the other one slide purposefully below her hips.

'Now,' he said, 'let's have no more nonsense about can't swim.' He tipped her briskly off her feet and up-ended her. 'Just do what I tell you and put your face in the water——'

'No!'

Elf's scream of panic raised heads all around the pool, and a couple cavorting at the deep end began to swim swiftly towards them.

'What the hell's the matter?' Richard's voice was brusque as he stood Elf upright again. 'I'm not going to hurt you, for heaven's sake.'

She was backing away from him, her big eyes wide and terrified. 'No,' she cried again. 'No, please. Don't...'

Richard tightened his lips and glared at her white, scared face. 'Stop it,' he said, recognising the need to dispel a totally irrational fear. 'Stop it at once, Elf. I'm not going to drown you.'

He saw her eyes widen again. 'Drown?' she croaked, her gaze transfixed like that of a hypnotised bird. Her words came out in short, breathless gasps. 'No. I'm sorry. I know you're not...' She wiped a hand over her eyes. 'I remember now. You're *that* Richard, aren't you? The one who—who pulled me out of the water, that day down by Ashburton Creek...'

CHAPTER FOUR

'HELL,' said Richard.

Elf moistened her lips, conscious that curious onlookers were staring. 'I—you—you're the boy who lived next door to us, aren't you?' she whispered to the grim-faced man beside her. 'From when I was seven. Only your name wasn't Laslo then . . .'

Richard pushed a hand through his golden-wet hair. 'Yes, it was. But you're right. Most people called us by my father's pen name. I was wondering when you'd remember.'

'And you wish I hadn't.' Elf's voice grew stronger. Her initial panic was subsiding. This was the Atlantic Ocean, not a man-made creek at the bottom of a Los Angeles garden—and Richard had never meant her any harm. She glanced at the gawking little crowd treading water at a discreet distance, and felt foolish—which, unreasonably, made her angry with the source of her discomfort, who was smiling with very little warmth.

'Not at all. I tried to tell you an hour ago. But you mistook my intentions for what my grandmother would have called a highly improper suggestion.'

Elf's mouth fell open. 'You don't—oh, no! You don't mean *that's* what you wanted to talk to me about...?'

'Of course it was. But your mind seemed set in a direction which I found...interesting—shall we say?—but not altogether complimentary. Later, if I'm not mistaken, you suggested a more permanent liaison.'

'Oh.' His tone was so caustic, so disparaging, that Elf dropped her head and buried her face in her hands.

Richard said nothing, and after a while she began to wonder if he was still in the pool. Then, after more time had passed, she stopped feeling foolish and started to feel angry instead.

This whole idiotic situation would never have arisen if Richard had levelled with her from the beginning, and she wouldn't now be standing in the water feeling a lot like the only whale in the pod who couldn't swim—with all the other whales looking on.

'Why didn't you tell me right away?' she demanded, belligerent now as she lowered her hands and glared up at Richard, who, as she might have known, was still very much in the pool and looking down at her with a flinty little smile.

He didn't answer at once, and, when he did, Elf noticed that his tone was unusually flat. 'Because to the best of my recollection the last time we met you told me you'd never speak to me again.'

'I was only eleven.'

'I know. A very angry eleven. In view of what happened after, I thought you might find the circumstances—awkward. I decided it would be best if you came to terms with the memory on your own.'

'Why should...? Oh.' Elf stopped and put a hand to her mouth.

Yes, she remembered now. And Richard was right. The circumstances had been awkward. Because, according to her parents, Richard had saved her life. And she had repaid him by refusing to speak to him.

She stared at the odd shape of his feet in the blue water. 'I remember now,' she said, not looking at him, but talking very fast. 'You were chasing me because I'd called you a name—several names—and you caught me, and I pulled away from you and slipped into the creek. I went under, and caught my foot in some weeds. I was struggling, terrified. Then I blacked out, didn't I? My parents said you dragged me out of the water and revived me—mouth to mouth.' She glanced at his lips and then looked quickly away.

'But you didn't believe them.' His voice registered an aloof disinterest that made her shrivel up inside.

She watched the drops of moisture form silver patterns on his golden skin. The crowd of onlookers in the water began to drift closer to the action. 'I did, I think,' she replied uncomfortably. 'But I couldn't forget that terrified feeling either, and I blamed *you*. We'd been arguing and you were mad at me. Really mad—and much bigger. I honestly thought that for once I'd pushed you too far. And anyway I was still furious with you.'

'I believe you had pushed me too far,' he said drily. 'But not to the point of leaving you to drown.'

'No. Of course not. I should have thanked you instead of refusing to see you.'

'Yes. You should.'

'What happened after that?' she asked slowly. 'I don't remember seeing you again.'

'You didn't. I went back to England with my parents two days later. You wouldn't talk to me. Or say goodbye.' Still that coolness, that slightly bored absence of feeling.

Elf frowned. It was all coming back to her now. 'I'm sorry,' she said slowly. 'I think I regretted it later. I—I missed you.'

'It hardly matters. You were only a child.'

'So were you. Fifteen is hardly grown up. I must have hurt your feelings very badly.'

He shrugged. 'I suppose I would have preferred grovelling gratitude, but, as everyone else assured me I was a hero, my ego wasn't damaged beyond repair.'

'That doesn't surprise me. Has it ever been?' The moment the words were out, Elf repented her unnecessary gibe.

Richard gave her a look that made her thankful they were still being watched from a circumspect distance. But all he said was, 'No, but it's been soundly battered a few times. Often by a spunky little sprite who was never afraid of anything—until that day she fell into the creek.'

Elf considered that. 'All right. But I still don't understand why you didn't tell me who you were right away.'

'I saw no reason to at first. Particularly as I suspected your memories of me were anything but positive—and very likely embarrassing.'

'Would that worry you?'

'Not in the least. You deserved to be embarrassed. But I wasn't sure I wanted to rake up a lot of childish nostalgia with a sharp-tongued young woman who——'

'Might feel she had some sort of claim on your attention.' Elf finished the sentence for him.

'Mmm. Something like that. But I changed my mind.'

'Why?'

He dropped a wet hand heavily on to her shoulder. 'I'm not at all sure. Perhaps I decided I ought to be rewarded for past gallantry.'

Elf splashed hastily out of his reach. 'You can just forget about...' She stopped. He was right in a way. He did deserve some sort of thanks—and an apology for this scene she had just created. It would have unbearably discomfited a lesser man.

'I do thank you, belatedly, for rescuing me,' she said solemnly, clasping her hands in front of her as if she were reciting her prayers. 'And I'm sorry I made such a commotion. It's just that when you told me to put my face in the water all my memories of that day came flooding back. I must have totally blocked it out, but for a moment there I felt as if I were a child again, slipping under the water, with you on the warpath, grabbing me...'

'Oh, I'm definitely on the warpath.' He was smiling now, but there was a curious edge to his voice that made Elf wonder if her thanks had been misplaced, and, because she was already feeling edgy and disturbed, she found it hard to control her irritation.

She raised her eyebrows with what she hoped was studied indifference. 'Well, now that we have that settled —— '

'What settled?'

Elf took a deep breath. 'That you saved my life. And that although I didn't grovel with gratitude for my rescue —— '

'An omission which can always be rectified,' he pointed out. 'I believe I'd enjoy a nice grovel.'

When he reached for her with a look in his eyes that was all too easy to interpret, Elf moved quickly out of his way. 'Don't you touch me,' she snapped.

'Why not?' Richard's tone was tinged with impatience. 'Don't you want to learn how to swim? Or are you wearing those delectable yellow Band-aids strictly for decorative purposes?'

'No,' said Elf. 'I mean, no, I don't want to learn how to swim. And my bathing suit is perfectly decent.'

'Did I say it wasn't?'

'No, but you're looking at me as if...'

'Yes?' He arched his eyebrows.

'As if...' Elf turned away. Without his even touching her, his slow gaze was ripping the narrow strips of cloth from her body, so that she stood exposed and vulnerable to him in the warm blue water.

'Elf,' he commanded, holding out his hand, 'come here.'

'No. I have to wash my hair,' she said firmly. She had had quite enough drama for one morning, and, even though there was something very seductive about Richard's outstretched fingers and his bronzed body gleaming above the water, she knew enough to get going while she could. Without looking back, she scrambled up the steps of the pool.

Behind her, she heard Richard give a short bark of laughter, followed almost at once by the unexpected sound of Miranda's distinctively high-pitched giggle.

Elf scowled, scooped up her towel, which had fallen on to the tiles, and padded off to the nearest lift.

Richard, discovering Miranda's hand gently caressing his shoulder, removed it without looking at her, and plunged swiftly under the water. When he surfaced, the beauty was stroking her way gracefully towards him.

'What an extraordinary girl Elf is,' she trilled derisively.

'Yes, isn't she? Quite extraordinary,' he replied coolly, taking care not to invite further comment. At this moment he was in no mood to discuss the companion of his childhood, especially not with Miranda, who smiled sweetly and tried another tack.

'I could do with a drink,' she hinted prettily.

'So could I,' he agreed, remembering Elf's comment that he was a fool to look a gift horse in the mouth. With a feeling of detachment, he observed the sexy wriggle of Miranda's rounded bottom as she clambered out of the pool. Felicity had had a nice figure. Very different from Elf's neat little body...

Richard frowned, and after a while he put his hands on the railing and pulled himself up beside Miranda.

Elf stared at her damp reflection in the mirror, and tried to understand what had happened. She shook her head, spinning a shower of small drops on to the carpet.

This was all becoming too much for her. The unwanted attraction she felt for a man who was too domineering and too cynical for her taste, her confusion when she realised how totally she had misread his intentions, the sudden revelation that they shared a past, and that he had kept it from her—even the minor pin-prick of Miranda's often aggravating presence... All of it was just too much.

And, to top everything off, sometimes she had a feeling that Richard regarded her as some sort of shipboard jester provided for his personal entertainment.

'It has to stop,' she muttered into the mirror. 'That's all there is to it. It *has* to stop.' Exactly what had to stop she wasn't sure, so she directed a fierce scowl at her dripping image and began to peel off her bikini.

Was it really fifteen years since a screeching little girl had squirmed away from Richard's avenging grasp and tumbled into the water?

As Elf wiped a cold trickle of water from her neck, she remembered the day Richard had arrived next door with his parents, after his father's lengthy novel had been shrunk into a Hollywood movie. Roger Laslo, determined to oversee the transition from script to screen, had brought his wife and son with him to Los Angeles. Elf, watching from a window, had seen Richard unfolding from a taxi, and been instantly smitten by his languid smile. Later, much to her satisfaction, the Laslos and the Makepeaces became friends, and, in spite of the difference in their ages, Richard and Elf had formed an uneven alliance too.

An unholy alliance, their parents had sometimes called it.

Unholy indeed, she thought wryly, dis-
carding her towel and zipping on her
primrose-yellow jumpsuit. Now more so than
ever. Because Richard was no longer a young
boy, but a man who had been married for nine
years. Tony had been married too, and any
woman who allowed history to repeat itself to
that extent was a blind fool.

'Which means that from now on, Elf
Makepeace, you will do your best to keep a
polite but definite distance from Richard
Laslo,' she informed an unresponsive wall as
she left the cabin.

A small emptiness opened somewhere close
to her heart.

Twenty minutes later she stepped round a
corner and found herself face to face with the
man she had vowed to avoid. He was wearing
white trousers and an open-necked shirt, and
he looked so lean and tempting that Elf had
to curl her fingers into her palms to stop
herself from reaching out to touch him.

Attached to his side like fungus was
Miranda.

All Elf's intelligent resolutions vanished on a cloud of red hair.

'Hi,' she said brightly, stopping squarely in front of them so they couldn't pass.

Miranda frowned, and Richard looked her up and down and asked pointedly, 'Finished washing your hair?'

As her hair was dry and fluffy as soft cotton following her adventure in the pool, Elf knew there was no sense in pretending.

'I changed my mind.'

'I thought you might.'

She sucked in the corner of her lip. Of course Richard had figured out that she had used her hair as an excuse to get away from him. But she wished he hadn't.

Before she could reply, Miranda said condescendingly, 'Richard and I are going for a drink, Elf, so if you don't mind...' She paused, waiting for Elf to take the hint and move.

Elf did mind. Quite alarmingly.

'Oh,' she said. 'A drink. Just what I need. Mind if I come too?'

'Delighted,' drawled Richard. He held out an arm and she took it, feeling suddenly foolish.

He sounded more bored than delighted, and Elf wished she had kept her mouth closed instead of attempting to crash his private party.

'On second thoughts,' she said breathlessly, as Richard strode down the passage to the bar with a woman trying to keep up on either side of him, 'maybe I don't want——'

'What don't you want?' Richard smiled with lazy innuendo. 'Me? Don't worry, I'm not on the menu.'

Elf took a deep breath and resisted the urge to slap his face. 'I didn't think you were.'

'Good, then stop behaving as if you imagine I'm likely to eat you. I prefer my hors-d'oeuvres on a plate, thank you, not over a bar stool. Besides, Miranda wouldn't like it. Would you, Miranda?'

Miranda looked as though she wouldn't mind what happened to Elf as long as it happened far away. 'But Richard, dear, if Elf says she doesn't want——'

'Elf often says things she doesn't mean, Miranda,' he told her grimly.

The beauty parted her rose-bud lips in a smile that showed too many teeth. 'I'd like a drink, please,' she said plaintively.

'Of course.' Richard handed her into a chair, then pulled out a second one for Elf, who accepted it with what she hoped he might take for weary condescension. She had lost enough dignity for one day. 'I'll have a lemonade,' she informed him.

'An excellent choice. Suitably temperate. Miranda?'

'I'll have the same.' Elf saw the other woman frown, and suspected she would have preferred something stronger.

She began to feel a little less foolish.

Richard lifted a finger to summon a steward.

'*Do* tell us something about yourself, Richard,' gushed Miranda as the drinks arrived. '*Are* you by any chance connected to Laslo's of Bond Street?' She manoeuvred her chair so that it cut off Elf's view of his face.

Richard eased his own chair sideways, restoring Elf's view and cutting off Miranda's. 'Yes,' he replied. 'You might say I'm connected.'

Miranda shuffled her chair again and leaned forward. 'Oh,' she breathed. 'You're not *the* Mr Laslo, are you?'

'If by "*the* Mr Laslo" you mean am I the current owner, the answer is yes.'

'Oh-h.' The redhead rolled her eyes up as if she'd just learned that Richard was the Archangel Gabriel. 'How exciting. And I've heard you're a *genius* at judging the value of gems.'

'Hardly a genius. The genius was my Uncle Julian who founded Laslo's.'

'Oh, yes,' said Miranda dismissively. 'He died, didn't he? A few years ago.'

'Yes.'

'Leaving the business to you?'

'That's right. He had no children and my father was only interested in his writing.'

'How lucky for you.' Miranda clapped her hands and laughed like an avaricious child.

'I didn't think so.' Richard's quietly civilised tone was cold as permafrost. 'Uncle Julian taught me all I know about the business. He was my friend as well as my partner. I'm afraid I didn't regard his death as any great cause for celebration.'

One in the eye for you, Miranda, thought Elf.

'*Well*, I didn't mean...' Miranda paused huffily, a calculating glitter in her eyes as she sought for a way to recover from her gaffe.

Elf tried to hide a smile in her lemonade. Miranda's parents might be in the market for a title, but it looked as though the bombshell herself was contemplating a much more permanent source of wealth.

She understood now who Richard Laslo was. Not just her old childhood ally, but the president of one of London's most prestigious jewellers. If she remembered correctly, Laslo's speciality was antique jewellery, but their modern pieces also had a world-wide reputation.

'Of *course* you wouldn't celebrate your uncle's death,' said Miranda, her downturned lips resuming their rose-bud pout. 'I just meant you must have been happy to inherit all that *gorgeous* jewellery... Oh, Richard, I would so love to visit your shop in London——'

'We're open Monday to Friday, ten till five,' he said crisply.

'Oh, but I meant a *private* viewing.' Her eyelashes fluttered beguilingly.

'We do private showings for special customers only.' He gave her a suave but unaccommodating smile.

Elf lowered her head, not wanting to witness the other woman's discomfiture after all. Richard was being his usual urbane self, coolly polite and civilised—but Miranda had made a grave tactical error in celebrating his Uncle Julian's death. There was a steely glint in his eyes that she wouldn't have wanted directed at herself.

Miranda didn't care for it either. 'Well!' she exclaimed. 'Well, really, Mr Laslo, I do believe you're trying to insult me.' She stood up and slung her bag on to her shoulder with a petulant shrug.

'Trying to?' Richard stretched his long legs and leaned carelessly back in a chair that suddenly seemed much too small for him. 'Whatever gave you that idea, Miss Bannington?'

'Oh!' Miss Bannington lifted a foot, and for a second Elf thought she was about to stamp it. 'Oh! I declare, I've *never* been spoken to like that in all my life. On the *Sunshine Ship* . . .'

Elf took a sip of lemonade and tuned the *Sunshine Ship* out. When she looked again, the indignant beauty was already marching out of the door.

'I've offended her,' remarked Richard, slinging an arm over the back of his chair and not sounding remotely repentant.

Elf stared at him and stood up. 'Yes, you have,' she said, trying not to betray a slightly guilty amusement. 'Not very clever of you, Mr Laslo.'

Richard whistled softly through his teeth. 'Oh, I don't know. I'm beginning to discover that curves, cleavage and baby-blue eyes don't necessarily make for scintillating company. Sit down, Elf.'

'No, I have to be going...'

'Why? To wash your hair again?'

The mockery in his eyes made Elf stiffen, and she lowered herself back into her chair. She would *not* let him think she was afraid of him.

'No, because I want to,' she snapped. 'And you shouldn't have got rid of Miranda. *She's* terribly impressed with you.'

'And you're not? I know, you've already made that crystal-clear, and somehow I've survived the disappointment. Incidentally, Miss Bannington is not in the least impressed with me. She's impressed with what she thinks I can give her.'

Elf went on glaring, but Richard, ignoring the glares, went on smoothly, 'On the other hand, I think *you* might appreciate the craftsmanship of some of my older pieces—for their beauty rather than their value.'

Elf, her gaze fixed woodenly on the bar, tried unsuccessfully to suppress a quick glow of pleasure at the compliment. Because, however much she fought it, there was something about this controlled, sophisticated man, with his passion for the cold beauty of jewels, that was more than just physical. He fascinated and absorbed her imagination even as she kept trying to fight the unwelcome attraction.

She remembered her earlier resolution to hold him at a distance, and had a horrible suspicion that if he gave her the opportunity that was one resolution she would break.

'Thank you,' she said, not meeting his eyes. 'It's kind of you to say so. Perhaps some day...' Her voice trailed off, and when he darted a sharp glance at her face she added hurriedly, 'Between the hours of ten and five, of course.'

Richard's lips twitched. 'Of course,' he agreed soberly.

Elf swallowed, flustered by the gleam in his eye. 'I do have to go,' she said uneasily. 'It'll be lunchtime soon.'

Richard nodded and rose with her. 'Yes,' he agreed, swinging his long torso round the table. 'Must keep our strength up, mustn't we?'

'Charles P. Waterbush always does,' observed Elf, pretending not to notice his sarcasm.

'Mmm,' agreed Richard gravely. 'I'm sure he has his cabin stocked with emergency sunflower seeds, grapefruit juice, celery and vitamins.'

In spite of herself, Elf laughed, which distracted a passing lady in red, who gave a little gasp and stumbled over a table leg.

Immediately Richard turned to help her, and, as he leaned forward to catch her arm, a photograph fell out of his pocket.

Elf picked it up off the floor.

It was the picture that had been taken of her as she boarded ship. The one in which she was posing as a fish.

'Where did you get this?' she asked, stunned, as the lady in red flushed deep pink and hurried away.

'From the ship's photographer. It's the one you said you didn't want for your children.'

'I know. I don't. But that doesn't mean *you* can buy it.'

'It does. I have.'

'But it's not yours.'

'It is now.' He held the picture at arm's length and narrowed his eyes. 'Yes, a bit fishlike,' he reflected. 'But then I'm fond of fish. On the whole I find it rather appealing. An appropriate souvenir of our shared past.'

'It's not supposed to be appealing.' Elf wasn't sure why she didn't want him to have the picture, but she knew she didn't. 'You can't keep it,' she snapped. 'It's mine.'

'Spoken just like the little girl I knew of old. Are you going to start calling me names now? If you do, I promise you I won't put up with it.'

He spoke lightly enough, but Elf heard the hard edge to his voice and knew he meant it.

She stared at the buttons on his shirt, horrified not with him but with herself. No, she wasn't going to start calling him names. Because he was right. She *was* behaving like a bratty kid. And she didn't really know why. At least—perhaps she did know. But she wasn't ready, didn't want to think about it too deeply. Not yet...

'Never mind. Keep it,' she said.

'I intend to.'

Elf looked up quickly. His face was more hawk-like than ever, and she felt an odd stirring of distress. Richard had her picture, but he spoke of it as a mere souvenir of the past—a past which was over and done with.

'Thank you for the lemonade,' she said grudgingly.

He didn't answer, and they left the green bar together in a silence which Elf found uncomfortable, and to which Richard seemed totally oblivious.

Elf sat on her bed listening to the creaking of timbers and scowling at a book on British castles. It kept dissolving into visions of Richard's face.

Why was it that he confused and irritated her so, one minute making her want to laugh, the next to kick him? As children they had quarrelled too on occasion, but they had understood each other. Sometimes she felt they still did. Yet she had been furious and disturbed that he'd bought her photo. It was almost as if he owned a piece of her...

She flipped a page. A piece of her... Yes, perhaps that was it... She didn't want Richard to claim any kind of hold. Or—oh, lord, maybe she did. Maybe that was the whole trouble. Elf groaned quietly. Of course he *was* horribly attractive, and the feelings he aroused were confusing. Strangely, Tony's rejection didn't seem as immediate any more. But Richard was the friend of her childhood, someone she had once loved in her own way. If she gave him her heart now, as a grown woman, instinct told her she would pay a far higher price. Sighing, she turned another page, stared down at the ruin of Restormel. As before, it turned into Richard.

She slammed the book shut.

When she glanced at her watch, she saw that somehow the whole afternoon had passed her by. And that was all Richard's fault too.

Half an hour later she was in the dining-room discussing the weather with Elizabeth. A few minutes after that, Richard strolled in, nodded coolly, and took his place beside her.

'Charming,' he murmured, as he raked his eyes over Elf's high-necked black and gold dress. 'You look like a wasp on her way to a nunnery.'

'Thank you,' said Elf. 'And I suppose you're the sinister black spider masquerading as a visiting monk.'

Richard put his glass down hastily and held a napkin up to his mouth.

'I'm beginning to think we could use some bug spray at this table,' remarked the irrepressible Jerry before Elizabeth could shut him up.

Miranda giggled, Richard smiled enigmatically, and Elf stared down at her plate. Charles P. Waterbush continued to demolish a breadstick.

'Elf,' said Miranda, breaking the silence that followed, 'you *are* odd, you know. Why wouldn't you let Richard teach you to swim?'

Before Elf could form a reply, Richard was answering for her. 'Sheer habit,' he explained to Miranda. 'There was a time in the lady's past when I wasn't her favourite person.'

'You still aren't,' said Elf, forgetting at once that she'd meant to remain distantly polite.

'I, on the other hand,' he continued as if she hadn't spoken, 'was delighted to meet my little friend again.' He draped an arm along the back of her chair, his fingers just touching her hair—and the provocative look in his eyes made heat start to smoulder in her toes and surge up to cover her ears. His deep, caressing voice did nothing to cool the turmoil in her blood either, especially when he added softly, 'That was a fascinating time we spent together. Don't you think so? I remember you made a most interesting suggestion.'

Elf gripped the edge of the table hard. 'Quite fascinating,' she agreed with cool uninterest.

Richard's dark eyebrows arched upwards. 'Particularly that time you managed to start my parents' car and drive it on to the road,' he said silkily. 'I was the one who got punished for it. And very painful it was, as I remember. Not at all thoughtful of you, my dear.'

Elf frowned, knowing he wasn't taking her to task for her long-ago misdemeanours, but for her much more current behaviour. 'You got your own back,' she pointed out. 'You chased me into the cherry tree, and, when I couldn't get down, you left me up there to die.'

'No, to miss lunch, I believe. Which undoubtedly did you good. But when I helped you down later you came at me like a little wildcat.' He smiled reminiscently. 'You haven't changed a great deal.'

A choking sound from Jerry's side of the table brought Elf back to the embarrassing realisation that they were not alone, and that three pairs of eyes were fixed on them with varying degrees of emotion. Jerry's were crinkled with laughter, Elizabeth's soft with sympathy, and Miranda's drawn together in a frown that detracted considerably from the classic perfection of her features.

Elf gave Richard a furious glare that was intended to reduce him to vapour, but only caused him to lift a languid eyebrow. Biting her lip, she turned her head away and pretended to be absorbed in the menu.

When, somewhere close to her ear, she heard a man's voice whisper a word that might have been 'witch', but wasn't, she ignored it.

It seemed a very long time before the meal, with all its uncomfortable undertones, was finally eaten. By that time Elf had decided that the dark anonymity of the movie theatre might suit her mood better than anything else this evening.

By the time she got there, though, the film had already started, and she groped her way to the nearest seat without stopping to think that she might not be the only one in search of anonymity. The story on the screen had been unfolding for almost ten minutes before it occurred to her that the long legs coiled much too close to her own were more than a little familiar. A warm, unexpected flush of desire mingled with a feeling of resentment that, of all the seats she could have chosen, she had picked this particular one.

'What are you doing here?' she demanded in a furious whisper.

'Watching this very dull movie,' Richard replied. 'How thoughtful of you to follow me. I can do with a little distraction.'

'I didn't...' said Elf.

'Didn't you?' She could tell he didn't believe her. 'Nevertheless, now that I *have* been distracted, I don't propose to watch it any longer. Come on. Time to go.' He stood up, pulling her with him.

For a few seconds Elf held back, but, as his fingers closed over her arm and he began to haul her past a row of muttering moviewatchers, she found she had no real inclination to resist.

Then they were standing under the bright lights of the lounge, and Richard's palm rested in the small of her back, pushing her ahead of him.

She stopped suddenly, and his body came up hard against hers, moulding itself to her small frame exactly as if it belonged there. She felt his arms circle her waist, then wrap themselves around her ribcage.

'Oh,' she gasped. 'What—why...?'

'Why did you stop?' he murmured into her ear.

'I don't know. Why are you doing this, Richard?'

'Doing what? I was under the impression *you* were the one who instigated this very welcome change of pace.'

'No, I——'

'And that being the case, Elfriede...' He rubbed a thumb tantalisingly down her side. 'That being the case, what do you suggest we do to pass the time?'

There was an unmistakable suggestion in his words, and Elf tried to wriggle away. But he only slid his hands down further to curl them with erotic effect around her hips.

'Well?' he asked, his tone soft, sensuous and hypnotic.

'I—I don't... Let's dance,' she managed to gasp. It was the only activity she could think of at this moment. The only safe one. What he would say if she tried to tell him it was her bedtime didn't even bear thinking of.

Richard laughed. 'All right. That will do for the present.' He spoke very softly, causing Elf to shiver even though the night wasn't cold.

As usual the dance-floor was vibrating with people and noise, and the band had long ago ceased its squeaking warm-up. The music was soft, slow, and, as the sea moved restlessly beneath them, Elf discovered that her vague dream of the day before had become reality. She was floating across the swaying floor, held expertly in a pair of long, masculine arms. The beat changed, became low and throbbing, shuddering up through the checkered floor. Richard drew her against him with cool efficiency, as if he were positioning her for the dance. All the same, the feel of his hard body made her gasp, and she wondered if she would ever breathe again. Then it didn't matter, because she didn't want to breathe again. Ever.

'I'm sorry I left you in the tree,' he said lightly. His cheek was just touching her hair, and his low voice caressed her like expensive silk. After a while he added, 'It had the desired effect, though, as I remember.'

'Probably,' she agreed, aware that once again he was using the past to make a point about the present. 'I'm sorry I stole your parents' car.'

'Mmm. One day I'll have to make you pay for that.'

Elf looked up at once, wondering if he was serious, but when she saw the taunting curve of his lips she looked away—and immediately caught sight of Miranda, who was slinking round the floor in a dress made of a clinging white fabric that flowed around her body so that every seductive line of it was revealed. She looked nearly naked and very lovely.

'I'm not paying for anything,' muttered Elf, remembering Richard's comment about her demure and nun-like black and gold. 'And anyway, you were a horrible little boy.'

He smiled lazily. 'Was I?'

The smile did strange things to Elf's stomach as cool green eyes scanned her face. For the first time, she noticed faint lines grooved at the corners of his mouth. Lines which reminded her that his life had not been one long round of sunshine, beaches and successful conquests. It had once included a wife—whom he'd lost.

'Well, maybe not *always* horrible,' she admitted without much conviction.

'Perhaps,' he said smoothly, 'it's time you found out just exactly how horrible I can be.'

'What do you mean?'

'I mean that from now on I expect a little more respect from you, young lady.'

'Respect . . . !' she choked, then broke off as Richard began to move his hands slowly over her back. Elf gave a small shiver as darts of desire shuddered up her spine.

'Respect,' he repeated gravely, 'for your elders and betters.'

'Elders and *what*?' she demanded. 'If you think...' She stopped, gasping, as the dance came abruptly to an end and Richard's hands moved below her waist.

'Think what?' he asked softly.

'That I'm about to respect the most arrogant man... Richard, take your hands off——'

'Off your delectable person? Certainly.'

The lights went up at that moment, and Richard released her unhurriedly, tucking her hand in his arm as he led her across to the bar.

Elf perched herself on one of the tall stools and eyed him with a mixture of indignation and admiration. She had to admit that he did look superb lounging against the counter in evening dress. Powerful, all male, not the sort of man one would care to cross. But she was about to cross him anyway, she suspected— or at any rate call his bluff. Richard was altogether too high-handed, too sure of himself. It was time someone cut him down to size. If that were possible.

'Strange, isn't it,' she murmured, staring pensively at a glittering painted mirror. 'Strange that after all these years we should meet again. And just happen to be at the same table.'

'Fate,' said Richard laconically.

'Fate?'

He shrugged. 'That and a few words in the right quarter. I had my table reservation changed when I discovered Elfriede Makepeace was on board.' He gazed blandly at a row of green bottles behind the bar.

'I thought so,' said Elf, surprised that he had so readily admitted it. 'Why?'

'Because I was curious to find out if you were still as much trouble as you used to be. And I found out to my cost that you are. You've also developed an unpleasantly sharp tongue in your pretty head. But then you always did need a firm hand.' He drummed his fingers on the counter-top and raised his glass.

'Huh. Yours, I suppose?' scoffed Elf, who could imagine where that hand would be placed.

'Preferably.' He looked her over with a cool, suggestive appraisal that made her blush.

'Have you quite finished?' she demanded, when his gaze at last came to rest on her face.

'For the moment.' He smiled with such magnetic sensuality that, in spite of her exasperation, Elf had trouble preventing herself from smiling back.

'I believe you could sell sunlight to vampires,' she said grumpily, wishing she could smother the small, hungry flames that continued to flicker inside her as she watched him lean over the bar. 'But then you always were——'

'Yes, I know. A horrible little boy.'

Elf sighed and sipped at her drink. 'Mmm,' she said. 'I suppose that's why we got along so well. Most of the time.'

'Because *you* were a horrible little girl?' he asked drily.

'Something like that.'

Richard's mouth tipped up in a wry grimace. 'Don't remind me,' he said feelingly. 'In your case, the more things change, the more they stay the same.'

Elf lowered her eyelashes so he couldn't read her intent, and aimed a deliberate kick at the long leg propped up on the foot-rest.

The muscles in Richard's jaw tightened a fraction and he leaned forward to flip a dark curl behind her ear. 'Watch it,' he warned, his lips very close to her neck. 'The last time you kicked me, I seem to remember boxing your ears.'

'You tried to,' agreed Elf, pulling a face at him. 'But my father caught you just in time.'

'So he did.' He straightened slowly. 'Next time you may not be so lucky. In the meantime, come and dance with me again.'

'That sounds like an order.'

'It is.' He caught her elbows, leaving her no time to point out that she didn't take orders, as he pulled her peremptorily off her perch and on to the dance-floor. The band was just tuning up again.

She thought of squirming away, but she felt drugged now, drowsy, unable to escape from Richard's arms. And behind her unusual lethargy was the unwanted knowledge that it would take just one very small move on his part to precipitate the very thing she didn't want to happen: a coming together that would fill her night with ecstasy and her morning with unbearable regret.

She sighed and rested her cheek on his chest. Somehow she was certain Richard wouldn't be making that move—and the most disturbing aspect of *that* was that she didn't, at this moment, know if she was glad or sorry.

'It's late,' she whispered when the dance ended.

'Off to bed now, are you, Cinderella?'

She looked up quickly, the taunting words bringing her back to reality, and instilling a healthy dose of common sense.

'No,' she said. 'I'm off to the powder-room. I don't even own a glass slipper.'

'Just as well,' drawled Richard.

Elf paused. 'Why?'

'Because I have no intention of scouring the ship for its owner.'

'That,' said Elf pertly, 'is because *you* are no Prince Charming.'

She had the satisfaction of hearing him murmur, '*Touché,*' as she turned away.

When she returned to the nightclub, she didn't see Richard at first. Then she discovered him propped against the far wall with a drink in his hand, apparently watching a

young couple performing improbably in-
decent gyrations on the dance-floor.

She observed him quietly, knowing he
hadn't seen her, and after a while she realised
he didn't even see the gyrating couple. His
mind was continents away from this frantically happy place with its music and dancing
and determined pursuit of pleasure. Where it
was she had no way of knowing, but he
looked like a man who had lost something he
intended to get back. There was a ruthlessness
about the thin-lipped mouth that should have
frightened her, but instead she felt a quick
stab of sympathy, a longing to protect him
from himself that made her feel time had
slipped out of kilter, that she was eleven years
old again and loyally championing her hero.

Then Richard lifted his glass and swallowed
deeply, and Elf's mind returned to the present
to gaze with reluctant admiration at the
aristocratic column of his throat.

A swirl of filmy white fabric distracted her,
and she turned to look.

Miranda had also noted the solitary figure
standing against the wall. Slipping from the

arms of her officer escort, she was hurrying across the floor in pursuit of more promising quarry.

CHAPTER FIVE

ELF blinked. Was she seeing things? Miranda wasn't a woman who picked up on subtle rebuffs, but surely even *she* must be aware that Richard hadn't been altogether responsive to her charms.

It would be interesting to see how he responded to this further assault on his 'assets'. Lips quirking, Elf stepped round a portly gentleman in green checks in order to get a better view of the scene across the room.

Richard was still absorbed in his thoughts, and he didn't notice Miranda hurrying towards him. She was moving her head from side to side like a chicken eyeballing its feed.

Elf settled down to watch the unfolding scene—then suddenly, and without pausing to analyse her motives, she was galvanised into action. Speeding past Miranda's abandoned partner, she darted round the chequered floor in time to see the redhead step up to Richard and touch his arm.

'Yes?' Elf heard him say with cool precision. And then, as he returned to his surroundings and realised who was accosting him, 'Ah. Miranda. We meet again.'

Miranda giggled coquettishly. 'Yes, and I *do* hope you're feeling better now,' she cooed.

'Better?'

'Well, yes. You *were* just a little bit grouchy this morning, weren't you?'

'Was I? I wasn't aware of it.'

'Weren't you? Oh, dear.' The beauty sounded flustered, but that didn't mean she was willing to accept defeat. 'Poor Richard,' she murmured sweetly. 'All by yourself again? How dull for you.'

'Not at all. I find my own company relaxing.'

You must be the only one who does, thought Elf, not quite believing what she was hearing.

'Oh, of course,' gushed Miranda. 'But surely a man like *you* won't want to spend the night *relaxing*.'

Elf couldn't see the long eyelashes batting their stuff, but she knew they were, and she shook her head in disbelief.

Richard pushed his hands deep into the pockets of his trousers, smiled enigmatically, and said, 'That depends.'

Elf didn't give Miranda time to ask, 'On what?' She knew Richard hadn't seen her, but, as she observed the carefully blank expression on his face, and the provocative way Miranda was tilting her head, a sudden crazy impulse propelled her forward. Without stopping to think, she walked up behind the temptress, tapped her on the shoulder, and said, 'Don't worry, Miranda. Mr Laslo already has plans for some energetic activity this evening. As well as a nostalgic trip down memory lane. Did you know he was a horrible little boy?'

Miranda's mouth displayed a good deal of gaping pink gum. When she realised that Richard was eyeing it with amazement, she shut it again, swallowed, and replied with an obvious effort, 'Oh, I'm sure he wasn't, Elf. *My* experience with dear Richard has been *quite* different.'

And if you flutter those eyelids again I may blacken them, thought Elf, who was beginning to realise what she might have let herself in for.

Miranda, not one to give up easily, turned her smile up another notch and murmured coyly, 'Perhaps tomorrow, then, Richard? It's so sweet of you to entertain Elf. I *do* hope her reminiscences don't exhaust you.'

'So do I,' said Richard. 'On the other hand, she did mention more—er—energetic activity.'

Miranda stopped smiling and turned away. Elf watched her glide seductively back to her officer with her tail by no means tucked between her legs, and she was surprised to find herself feeling almost sorry for the retreating beauty. It couldn't be easy being Miranda, who would probably never learn that looks weren't an automatic passport to popularity.

After that she stopped thinking about Miranda, because Richard had placed a finger under her chin and was tilting it up so that she was forced to look into his eyes. 'And what was that about?' he asked conversationally. 'Did you decide I needed rescuing from an unrelaxing night in the arms of our resident siren? If that's the case, I presume you have a substitute in mind?'

Elf stared at him, not sure if he was teasing or serious, and not at all sure what had come over her. 'No, of course I haven't,' she said quickly, feeling heartily thankful for the dim lighting. 'And you didn't need rescuing, did you?'

'I wasn't about to accept the lady's offer, if that's what you mean.'

Elf blinked. His voice had turned unexpectedly cool, as if she had accused him of something odious.

'It wouldn't be my business if you had,' she said firmly.

'I'm glad you realise that.'

'Yes. Well, what I really meant was——'

'That I could have extricated myself without your assistance? Yes, I could. But I wouldn't have enjoyed it nearly as much as watching you go into action.'

Elf took a deep breath. His voice was even now, his features carefully blank, but she was *almost* sure he was laughing at her. And she didn't like it. It made her feel young and naïve.

'I'm sorry I interfered,' she said, hoping her hurt didn't show. She smiled brightly and held out her hand. 'Goodnight, Richard.'

'*Goodnight*,' he repeated. 'But I understood we had plans for some *energetic* activity this evening. Followed by a nostalgic tête-à-tête about our past. Or possibly the other way around.'

He took her outstretched hand and held on to it, and Elf was horrified to read determination in the inflexible slant of his mouth. As if he had made a decision and meant to act on it. She had a feeling she was the decision. The thought excited her and scared her at the same time.

She shook her head, unable to believe she had got herself into this mess. 'That was just—just something to say,' she mumbled, wishing his touch would stop sending shock waves up her arm.

'To disentangle me from Miss Bannington's clutches? Ah, yes, but they were very attractive clutches, don't you think? You owe me one, Makepeace.'

'I don't. You said you didn't—didn't mean to accept her offer.' She removed her hand from his grasp and looked him straight in the eye. 'Thank you for a pleasant evening, Richard.'

'Pleasant?' he said, cool and softly sarcastic. 'Yes, I suppose it was that. But why settle for green cheese when you can have the moon?'

Elf heard the faint note of mockery, assessed the thin curve of his lips, and wondered if he was baiting her or if he truly thought she would end up tumbling obligingly into his bed.

'You're hardly the moon, if that's what you mean,' she said drily.

He laughed. 'I can always count on you to cut me down to size, can't I, Elf? As it happens, that wasn't what I meant at all. Rather the opposite.'

Elf stared at him, puzzled and disconcerted. She was still trying to decide if he was flattering, flirting or making an impertinent suggestion, when he touched her on the cheek, said, 'Goodnight, Lady Moon,' and disappeared through the nearest exit.

Elf gazed after him, frowning. What in the world was going on in his mind? For that matter, what was happening to hers? She started to wend her way round the crowded dance-floor, intending to return to her cabin. Then she hesitated. Why should she go tamely off to bed? She wasn't likely to sleep anyway, and somewhere out there the moon was shining, and the ocean was dark and filled with dreams...

Her mind made up, she hurried out on to the deck. A pale grey fog had drifted in during the course of the evening, and now she could scarcely see the rail. Pulling her thin wrap around her shoulders, she stared blindly out into the mist.

'I expect the *Sunshine Ship* would have ordered better weather, don't you?' murmured a mischievous voice in her ear.

Elf jumped, as Jerry, his puckish face creased in a conspiratorial grin, loomed out of the fog beside her. 'Glad to see you getting some fresh air,' he said approvingly. 'You looked a little peaky at dinner.'

'Did I?'

'Mm. Not unhappy in love, I hope?' The bright little eyes were fixed on her with friendly concern, and Elf wished they were not so perceptive.

'No, of course not,' she replied quickly.

'I'm glad. Richard Laslo is an interesting young man, but I'd say there's a good deal of steel beneath the velvet.'

Elf smiled. 'Yes, you're right. But I'm used to it. He was like that when I knew him as a child.'

Jerry nodded. 'I suspected that. Don't let him hurt you, my dear.'

'I won't,' Elf assured him.

But as they walked the deck together in companionable silence she wondered if she'd be able to keep her word. She remembered how Tony had pressured her to share his bed, how she had wanted to give in to him in a way, because it had seemed a way to be closer. She had longed for closeness... But years ago she had resolved to wait until marriage for that greatest of all human intimacies, and, surprisingly, she hadn't found it all that hard to stick to her guns.

Richard was different. Richard was an aphrodisiac, as addictive as any drug and more dangerous. Because she wanted him with a hunger that was almost a hurt. She wasn't sure what she felt about him as a man, and it didn't matter, because she knew that all he felt for her was amused affection and a blatantly physical urge to take her into his bed. Richard didn't believe in the existence of the kind of love that changed lives and lasted

'till death us do part'. He had called that kind
of love a fantasy.

But she believed in it.

In spite of Harry, in spite of Tony, she had
managed to hold on to a dream. If she allowed Richard to become that dream, Elf
sensed that those previous hurts would
eventually seem like mere pin-pricks.

'Penny for them.' Jerry's voice jarred her
out of her musings.

'I was—I was just thinking that it's warm
in spite of the fog,' replied Elf, who hadn't
been thinking anything of the sort.

'Hmm.' Jerry eyed her shrewdly, but didn't
pursue the matter, and Elf realised that her
uncertain state of mind must be obvious to
anyone with eyes in his head. Which meant
she had better throw herself so whole-
heartedly into the activities of the ship from
now on that everyone on board would assume
she was having the time of her life. There was
no point in worrying her new friends.

It wasn't until much later the following day
that it occurred to Elf that attending a talk
entitled 'How the Stars Can Help You Select
a Mate' was perhaps not the best way to convince the world that her heart was whole and

intact. But by then she had slept through most of the lecture in any case.

She decided she would have to manage her love-life without the help of astral intervention.

That evening, she arrived at the traditional captain's party dressed in her yellow silk dress with the almost indecently long slit up the back, and was comforted to see more than one male eye light up as she entered the lounge.

Richard wasn't the only fish in the ocean. Not that she was interested in fishing, she reminded herself hastily.

After she had run the gauntlet of ship's officers assembled to shake an endless procession of hands, she began to search the room for familiar faces. At once her gaze fell on Richard. Never an easy man to miss, he was leaning against a pillar with his arms crossed, and he looked remote and little forbidding. She remembered that today would have been the tenth anniversary of his marriage.

Elf hadn't seen him all day, and, just to prove to herself that she was capable of carrying on a casual conversation with him without going all liquid inside, she edged round a group of awestruck teenagers and strolled up to him.

At once the remote look vanished, and a white smile slashed the contours of his striking face. The suggestive gleam in his eyes as he ran them boldly over the dress that revealed everything and nothing at the same time told her that the two weeks' salary she had spent on this little number had been well worth it. Perhaps too well worth it.

'Don't move,' he commanded, as she leaned towards him. Mesmerised, she had swayed so close that she could feel his warm champagne breath on her cheek.

'Why ever not?'

'Because if you keep still, I can just about control the primitive urges that dress inspires. Move, and I won't be responsible for the consequences.'

Elf smiled uneasily. 'Do you like it?'

Suddenly she knew exactly what the term 'bedroom eyes' meant, as his smouldering green gaze came to rest on her breasts where they strained against the smoothness of silk. She felt as if he were undressing every inch of her and that she stood naked for his eyes alone.

'*Like* is not the word,' he said, in that deep, seductive voice that sent shivers down her spine. He lifted his arm to curve long fingers possessively round the back of her neck. The emerald intensity of his gaze held her pinioned, unable to breathe. Something flared in her then that was more than just lust, and for a moment she was sure he felt it too.

Then a nasal voice behind them squawked disgustedly, 'Cheap, isn't it?'

And the moment passed.

'What's cheap?' asked Elf huskily, as she came back to earth with a thump.

'This alleged champagne. It's just cheap wine with bubbles.' Miranda flicked the edge of her glass contemptuously, and took a sip.

'I shouldn't complain; it's on the house.' Richard's voice was dry, bordering on abrupt.

Elf glanced at him quickly. Was he too having trouble descending from the clouds? No, of course he wasn't. She dismissed the thought at once. He was just being his cynical self.

'On the *Sunshine Ship* we had Cordon Rouge,' Miranda sniffed.

Elf didn't care what they'd had on the *Sunshine Ship*. Neither, apparently, did

Richard. As a man with a drooping moustache and a Rolex watch came up to claim
Miranda's attention, he took Elf's elbow and
murmured into her ear, 'Come on. We're
getting out of here.'

'But I only just arrived.'

'So did I.'

'But —— '

'Don't give me buts, Elf. I'm tired of trying
to talk sense to you surrounded by seven
dozen gawping strangers.'

Elf started to say she didn't want him to
talk anything to her, especially sense, and that
she was quite happy where she was, thank
you. But Richard was holding her elbow,
manoeuvring her past the line of smilingly
stiff-lipped officers as well as Charles P.
Waterbush, who didn't see them because his
gaze was fixed glumly on a very small hors-
d'oeuvre clasped between his thumb and fat
forefinger. She could feel Richard's thigh
against her hip, the firm pressure of his fingers
on her elbow—and she found herself walking
beside him without protest, allowing him to
lead her from the room.

Once away from the chattering celebrants,
Richard settled himself in a turquoise love-

seat by a tall window overlooking the ocean, and, without being asked, he scooped her on to his knee.

'What are you doing?' gasped Elf. 'Richard, what's this all about?'

'Us,' he replied. 'This.'

As she gaped at him, trying to make sense of what was happening, he put his hand on the back of her head, tipped her face up and kissed her.

She was too startled to resist, and it was over before she had time to gather her wits.

'What did you do that for?' she asked, leaping to her feet and backing against the window with one fist pressed against her heart. It sounded like a drumbeat in her ears.

'In a dress like that, surely you expected to be kissed,' Richard drawled. 'The invitation was too tempting to ignore.'

'Oh! You—you...'

He shook his head. 'Don't waste time calling me names, Elf. I said I wanted to talk to you. I meant it.'

'We have nothing to talk about,' said Elf.

'Oh? Not even our shared past?'

'Well, I...' Her voice trailed off.

'You haven't an answer for that, have you? What is it with you, Makepeace? I've apparently been forgiven for my thoughtlessness in dragging you out of Ashburton Creek, so why continue to behave as if you think I'd as soon rape you as look at you? I assure you that's not something I do.'

'I know. I didn't think...' Elf swallowed, pressed her palms against the cold glass of the window. Plain speaking was the only thing that would work with Richard Laslo. It always had been.

'I've just got over a man who said he loved me when he didn't,' she told him, turning to stare out at the ocean as she tried to control the quiver in her voice. 'I'm in no hurry to have my heart broken again.'

'But I haven't told you I love you, have I? And I've no plans to break your heart, Elfriede.' He sounded impatient, even a little bored.

'No, I don't suppose you have. I doubt if you'd even know you were doing it.'

'Is that what you think of me?'

Elf saw his nostrils flare improbably, and his mouth harden, and she knew that there was no point in trying to explain how she felt.

Richard had been contentedly married to a woman who had been his childhood friend. But it had been a marriage of affection and habit, not of passion. He wouldn't understand about heartbreak.

'Yes, it's what I think of you,' she said, pushing herself away from the window. 'So I don't think there's any more to be said.'

'Don't you?' said Richard. 'What a naïve little creature you are. You really *believe* in fairy-tales, don't you?' He smiled in a way that made her flinch. 'Whatever will you do when you grow up and discover that Prince Charming doesn't exist, Elf? That you'll have to settle for a flesh and blood man?' When she only stared at him, hurt and stunned, he added roughly, 'Oh, run back to your party, Cinderella.'

Elf didn't run. She walked away with dignity, her head held high, and returned to the captain's party. She was not going to miss it altogether just because one handsome, arrogant man had pulled her on to his knee and kissed her—and then told her to run away.

Her eyes glazed over as she gazed at the packed crowd of revellers shuffling around the thick red carpet, and when she hesitated she found herself tripping over a trunk-like leg which Charles P. Waterbush had extended to waylay a passing tray of sandwiches and olives. A waiter pressed champagne into her hand as she looked up at Charles to murmur a rueful apology.

'You'll break it if you're not careful,' he warned her, waving a sandwich in the direction of her fingers. She glanced down and saw that she was squeezing the stem of her glass as if it were a tube of toothpaste.

Elf flashed him an empty smile, and swallowed the rest of her drink in one gulp. Then she put down the glass and left the room.

Fresh air, she thought groggily. That's what I need. Not the clatter and crush of a party.

It wasn't very fresh, though, only damp and cold, and the clinging silk felt clammy against her skin. But now, away from the warmth and champagne, her drifting thoughts sharpened and became clearer.

She was behaving like a confused and moonstruck adolescent, one minute responding to Richard, even pursuing him, the next trying to hold him at bay. And, if one didn't count that time out of their childhoods, she had known him for precisely three days. Sure, time and emotions tended to get distorted on board ship, but that wasn't much excuse for what was happening. Richard was impossibly sexy and attractive when he wasn't being cold and cutting. But he didn't believe in what he called fairy-tales, and he hadn't given her the remotest reason to think he regarded her as more than a possible bedmate.

As she didn't want that kind of loveless union, there was nothing to be moonstruck about.

A strand of damp hair tickled the corner of her eye and she brushed it away impatiently. Her hands were wet from holding on to the rail, and the cold was beginning to chill her through and through. She turned to go back inside.

The party would be over by now, and the passengers streaming in to dinner. Elf squared her shoulders. Tonight she would ignore Richard Laslo and concentrate on her food.

Fifteen minutes later, when Richard strode into the dining-room, he was startled to see the lone occupant of his table glaring malevolently at a large basket of crusty rolls. His

eyes glittered, and the smile which lit his face
was not benevolent.

'Hello, daffodil,' he said, coming up behind
Elf and ruffling her curly dark hair.

Elf stopped glowering at the rolls and
glowered at him. 'Daffodil?' she repeated
woodenly.

'Mm. You always dress in yellow—like a
daffodil. I like it.' He smiled with cool innuendo, as if their earlier conversation hadn't
happened. When their eyes met with a spark
of awareness that Elf refused to acknowledge, she clenched her knuckles briefly
on her napkin before turning back to the rolls.

'I'm glad you approve,' she replied, turning
her back.

Richard sat down, and noted that Elf was
displaying a sudden marked interest in the salt
and pepper shakers.

'Thinking of pocketing them for your collection?' he asked.

Elf shifted her attention to the water jug.

Richard's eyes narrowed as he reached deliberately across the table and lifted the jug to
fill her glass.

'Thank you,' said Elf, in a small, chilly
voice.

'My pleasure. Now, perhaps if you'd condescend to look at me...'

But Elf couldn't look at him. She wanted to in a way, but she knew that if she did, and if by chance he smiled that impossible smile at her, all her determined resolutions would probably crumble. Which ought to tell her something, she supposed. Something she didn't want to know...

Jerry and Elizabeth arrived then to cut off further private conversation. They were followed closely by Charles, but of Miranda there wasn't a sign. Probably dining with the Rolex watch, thought Elf without much interest.

All through her shrimp cocktail, Elf ignored Richard and chatted animatedly with Elizabeth and Jerry. When, during the salad, Richard murmured that he was glad to see she had a hearty appetite, she gave him a malicious glare and pointedly refused to answer.

Richard smiled without mirth and turned his attention to Elizabeth.

If Elf had been looking at him, she would have seen the hard green glitter in his eyes as he picked up a prawn and cracked it between his fingers. And if she'd seen it she might have been warned.

As it was, when dinner was over, she hurried into the ladies' room, and later, after making sure that Richard was nowhere to be seen, she tried to lose herself in the crowd near the cabaret. A comedian was strutting his stuff, and he was good. Normally Elf would have chuckled, but this evening she saw nothing to laugh at.

Feeling depressed and restless for no reason she was willing to acknowledge, she got up and strolled into the casino. She didn't expect to run into Richard there because she was almost certain he wasn't a gambler in the usual sense.

A collection of broad-shouldered dinner-jackets and backless evening gowns hunched hungrily over the tables. Around the edges of the room, slot-machines clicked and glittered as glassy-eyed patrons balanced drinks in one hand and mechanically pulled handles with the other. Every now and then someone shrieked greedily as coins clattered into a tray.

An intriguing spectator sport, thought Elf idly. She wasn't interested in trying it herself.

Which was just as well, seeing that she couldn't afford it.

After twenty minutes of trying to breathe in the stifling atmosphere, she began to find the smoke and heat too much to take. When her eyes began to smart, she turned to leave.

She was passing the last roulette table when two long legs appeared out of the blue in front of her. Having no choice, she stopped, forced to an abrupt and undignified halt by a pair of elegant black trousers. The owner of the trousers had his back to the table and was lounging against it with his arms crossed.

'And where do you think *you're* going to, my pretty maid?' asked Richard softly.

Elf stumbled, and only just managed to avoid falling on her face.

'I'm going to bed, if you must know,' she snapped. 'At least I was until your legs got in the way.'

Richard stood up, his figure seeming to tower above her beneath the pale glow of the lights.

'Feeling a little sour, are we?' he suggested, taking her arm in his firm grip. 'Keep it up, and I may have to do something to improve your temper.'

'Such as?' demanded Elf.

He smiled wickedly. 'Where did you say you were going?' he asked, as his eyes played over her figure with unmistakable meaning.

'Oh!' Elf bit her lip to keep back the furious retort that she knew would only incite him to further mockery. Who did he think he was anyway, this rude, arrogant... and maddeningly attractive man, who seemed to be bent on driving her to murder—or at least to drink? Just now she wished she had one to pour over his head.

As if he had read her thoughts, Richard continued smoothly, 'But perhaps I'd better postpone the pleasure for the present. You appear to need cooling down. I think I'd better buy you a drink.'

'I don't want a drink,' snapped Elf, who knew just what she'd do with it if she had one.

'Don't be tiresome,' he replied equably, putting his free hand in the small of her back and pushing her firmly across the room.

Elf thought of struggling, but his hand slid down lower and she gasped instead. People were already staring, and in the end she gritted her teeth and allowed him to urge her into a relatively quiet corner by the bar.

'Sit down,' he ordered. When she didn't move he turned her smartly around and deposited her in a black leather chair.

'It's a good thing these seats are padded,' muttered Elf, as he settled himself across from her and made a sign to the steward.

'What was that?'

'I said it's a good thing these seats are padded. I'm not made of sawdust, you know. I do have feelings in the part of me I sit on.'

'Do you, now?' Richard's gaze moved thoughtfully to the part in question, which was still perched awkwardly on the edge of the chair where he had put her. 'Yes, I seem to remember your parents were obliged to make use of that fact on occasion. When you didn't manage to shift the blame for your misdeeds on to me.'

'I didn't,' gasped Elf indignantly. 'I *never* tried to blame you.'

The corner of his mouth slanted crookedly. 'I know. But I was older and I got it anyway. As a matter of fact one of the things I always admired about you was your honesty. The two of us would incite the entire adult community to violence, and you, who could have got away with it, wouldn't even try to deny your guilt. Brave of you, of course, but very stupid.'

'You,' said Elf, contemplating violence herself, 'are without a doubt the most cynical and obnoxious man I've ever met. You haven't changed a bit since you were a boy.'

'Yes, I have,' replied Richard imperturbably. 'In those days you were a sweet kid, and I didn't want to marry you in the least. Now you're a sour-tongued daffodil—and I've decided I do.'

CHAPTER SIX

'WHAT?' Elf reached for the cold drink the steward had brought her, swallowed half of it, and choked.

Richard handed her his handkerchief with an air of pained resignation.

She accepted it and dabbed at her eyes. 'What are you talking about?' she demanded, most of the anger knocked out of her by his sheer audacity. He smiled impassively and didn't answer, so she added a forceful, 'Richard, I didn't think that was funny the first time. I still don't.'

His smile stretched, showing his teeth, and his hypnotic eyes didn't leave her face. 'It wasn't meant to be funny. I'll admit that when you suggested it——'

'*I* suggested it?'

'Mmm. Twice as a matter of fact. I suppose you're going to tell me you've forgotten.'

Elf was speechless.

He shrugged. 'In any case, I was about to say that when you first suggested it I was—

to put it mildly—taken aback. But, on thinking it over, I've come to see that the idea has a number of advantages.'

Elf tried to stand up and found she couldn't. She seemed to be glued to her chair. 'Why would you want to marry a woman you consider childish and naïve?' she asked finally, and with a touch of acid. 'Has the frog turned into a prince after all?'

'Not likely.' He gave her a twisted smile. 'I'm sorry if I offended you, Elf. The truth is, I find your innocence rather charming.'

'Why, how condescending of you, Mr Laslo.' Elf gave an affected little wriggle. When he didn't respond, she came down from her high horse and asked flatly, 'Why do you want to marry me?'

He pulled a silver pen from his pocket and tapped it abstractedly on the table. 'Why do men usually marry?'

Elf stared at him. His face was without expression now, and there was nothing to tell her whether her answer was important to him or not.

'Any number of reasons,' she said cautiously.

'I suppose so. Very well, take your pick.'

Suddenly all Elf's confused resentment congealed into one steaming knot of indignation that swelled up into her throat and threatened to choke her. If she didn't release it immediately she would explode.

'All right, I will,' she said through gritted teeth. 'I suppose you've decided a year is long enough to go without a permanent bedmate. You could settle for Miranda, of course, but possibly she's too much to take. Even for you. Or perhaps you've already sampled the wares —— '

'Perhaps I've *what*?'

Elf was too wound up to notice the thin white grooves beside his mouth, but she saw his lips flatten forbiddingly.

'Sampled the wares,' she repeated. 'Miranda's wares.' Even as she spoke, she knew that the charge was unfounded. Richard had danced with the beautiful redhead, admired her looks without cupidity, but that was all.

'Ah.' He stabbed the pen into a coaster. 'And what makes you think that, Elfriede? I must say, I don't find your estimate of my taste in bedmates especially flattering.'

Elf stared at his taut body coiled in the black leather chair, and, although it wasn't cold, she shivered. 'I wasn't planning to flatter you,' she said, curling her fingers tightly into her palms.

'So I gathered.'

'Not that your taste in women is any of my business,' she added belatedly, pointing her nose at what she hoped was a dignified angle.

'Hmm. So you remembered that.' He laid the pen on the edge of the table. 'However, if it will put your mind at rest, I don't mind telling you that although Miss Bannington seems most anxious to get her painted claws on Laslo's assets——'

'Well, I suppose you're one of those,' Elf conceded sourly.

Richard strummed his fingers on his thigh. 'Do you have to be deliberately fat-headed? I was *not* referring to myself. If I happen to go along with the stock, she'll take me too, but our Miranda's sights are set on more valuable prizes. As I was about to say, the lady may be on a fishing trip for a useful husband, but that doesn't mean I've taken the bait, and I don't much care for the implication.'

No, thought Elf. If I were you I wouldn't care for it either. Besides, it was a stupid thing to say because I didn't really believe it for a moment.

'I'm sorry,' she said, picking up her glass and muttering into it.

'What was that?'

Oh, of course he wasn't going to let her off the hook that easily. 'I said I'm sorry,' she repeated, lifting her head and looking him straight in the eye. 'For suggesting that you were a total opportunist. I do know better, but you made me angry.'

Richard nodded. 'Apology accepted. All right, now that we've got that out of the way, perhaps you can come up with some other reason why I might be misguided enough to want to marry you.'

Elf gaped. She seemed to gape a lot around Richard—and for a few moments there she had actually forgotten his inexplicable proposal. If it could be called a proposal. 'I suppose,' she said, staring at her reflection in the polished table, 'that it's too much trouble to find a wife in the normal way, so you think I'll do.'

'And why,' he drawled, putting the pen back in his pocket, 'would I be insane enough to think a sharp-tongued, suspicious, impudent little piece like you could possibly "do"?'

'I'm not —— ' Elf began. Then she stopped. No doubt that was exactly how he saw her. And her opinion of him wasn't much better. 'I've no idea,' she snapped.

'I didn't think you had. In that case I'll give you a few hints.'

'Hints?'

'Mm. Do you remember why we had that quarrel the day you fell into the creek?'

'No,' replied Elf suspiciously. 'What's that got to do with —— ?'

'Quite a lot. You asked me to marry you, and I refused.'

'I what?' Elf bent forward, caught the edge of the table. 'I didn't...'

'Yes, you did. And I laughed and said eleven-year-old girls couldn't marry, and that by the time you were old enough I'd probably have married someone else. So you lost your temper and kicked me hard in a most unfortunate place—by accident, I hope—which made me lose *my* temper —— '

'Yes,' said Elf slowly. 'I remember now. *That* was why you were so mad at me. Of course it was.'

'Mmm. I told you we had some unfinished business.'

'What do you mean?'

'You asked me to marry you. It's a little late, I grant you, but I've made up my mind to accept.' He tipped his chair back and smiled as if he expected delighted thanks.

'Don't be ridiculous,' said Elf. 'I was just a child.'

'I know. But you had the occasional sensible idea even then. Besides, you repeated the offer. On the whole, I prefer being married to not, and as I've known you for a very long time I've no doubt I can keep matters on track——'

'By "matters", I suppose you mean me.'

'Precisely.'

'But luckily for me I'm not a train,' jeered Elf sweetly. 'What other inducements do you have?'

'Inducements?'

'To marry you, of course.'

'Ah. Well, for one thing you're quite right. I would like to take you to bed.' He bent forward, picked up her hand, and began to stroke the inside of her wrist. 'And, whatever you may be about to say to the contrary, that's a compliment, Miss Makepeace. Also I have a feeling you'd like it too.'

Elf felt the colour flaming over her cheeks. 'You *are* sure of yourself, aren't you?' she scoffed. 'I wonder if it would surprise you to know that I'm possibly the only woman you've ever met who *doesn't* find you irresistible. You're the last man in the world I'd want to find beside me in the morning.'

It wasn't true, of course. Just the thought of waking to find Richard beside her, his hands exploring her body, sent a hot quiver sizzling through her veins.

She looked up to see his ice-green eyes penetrating her defences. He *knew*, she realised. He knew exactly what she'd been thinking. She bit her lip.

Richard gave her his Mr Cool smile, dropped her hand, and continued as if she hadn't spoken. 'Another hint. I know you want children some day. You told me so. So do I. Very much. And Felicity and I—didn't have any.'

Elf, who had been gearing up for battle, heard a note in his voice that the dispassionate words couldn't quite hide. He actually cares, she thought. Having a family really matters to him. Maybe he even *likes* children. She swallowed the words she had been about to spit at him and said, 'I'm sorry about that,' instead.

He brushed her sympathy aside. 'We adjusted to it. But in the circumstances I see no reason why you and I can't come to an arrangement.' Taking her completely by surprise, he reached across the table to cup her chin.

Elf inched away from him. This was too much. Maybe Richard had needs just as she had, but how dared he suggest that she should marry him not because he loved her, but because he fancied her as a bed partner and he wanted children? I might as well be a cow to his bull, she thought bitterly, trying to get a grip on her temper. Not that he'd said that exactly, but how else was she to interpret his 'proposal'?

Somehow, she realised, this discussion must be brought to an end—quickly, and without causing a scene. She didn't like public displays of private problems any more than she imagined he did.

'I am not,' she said, her lips so close together that the words came out in a hiss, 'going to marry you, Richard Laslo.' There, that had to be clear enough. Even if in some traitorous part of her being she wished she could have given a different answer.

'Ah.' Richard linked his hands at the back of his neck. 'I see. Any special reason? Other than that I'm not irresistible?'

Elf was too overwrought to care about the way his voice grated over the words, but she recognised the cynicism behind them. He really saw nothing wrong with marrying her for physical satisfaction, companionship when it suited him, and the chance to produce a family. Perhaps he thought all marriages were like that. But they weren't. She knew better. Her parents had been a shining example of married love.

Elf took a long breath and eventually managed to reply, 'Yes. A number of reasons. One, you don't love me—and I don't love you.' She added that hastily, wishing she had said it first. 'Two, I don't want to marry you or anyone else. Three, you're an overbearing, conceited chauvinist and you think you just have to raise a finger to have any woman you want fall all over you—and four, I don't even like you.' She stopped, having run out of inspiration.

'Don't you? I thought you did.'

'You what?' Elf's eyes widened.

'I thought you liked me,' he repeated. Heavy lids formed a hood over his eyes. 'I've always liked *you*—for some reason which at this moment eludes me.'

'You can't be serious!' she exclaimed.

'I am, though. I still think you like me.' He shrugged. 'But it seems I haven't handled this business as well as I might have...'

'I'm not a *business* to be handled,' said Elf frigidly.

His smile was bleak. 'Did I suggest you were?'

'It sounded like it, and if you're going to go on being a jerk I'm leaving.'

'There's nothing to stop you,' he said evenly.

But there was. His hard gaze pinned her in her chair, and she couldn't have moved if she'd tried.

'There is one thing I'd like to make clear before you go,' said Richard, as she struggled to break contact with his eyes.

Unexpectedly, life returned to her paralysed limbs. 'No, I've heard enough,' she said shortly. 'Goodnight.'

Ignoring the lift, she made a bee-line for the stairs, and stumbled down to Deck Three as though all the demons of hell were in pursuit. But it wasn't until she reached the door of her cabin that she realised her own particular demon was right behind her.

'Look,' Richard said, grabbing her wrist as she tried to fit the key in the lock, 'I know you don't want to, but you're damned well going to listen to me, Elfriede.'

He was very close, his breath warm on her cheek. She could feel the length of his body along her back. When she turned, he didn't move away, and his thighs pressed her to the door as she faced him. Desire flared like lightning, quick and unbidden, and she raised her eyes.

'All right,' she said in a strangled voice. 'Talk, then.' She had no alternative but to listen now. The feel of his body thrusting against hers had dissolved the last vestige of her will-power.

'Open your door, then.' He took his hand from her wrist and gestured at the key in her hand.

'No.' Some remnant of control returned now that he'd released the pressure. 'Say what you want to say here. Quickly. And then I'm going to bed—alone.'

His lips twisted. 'Right. If that's how you want it.' He moved forward again, his thighs once more holding her against the door, and she knew that wasn't how she wanted it at all. She didn't want to go to bed alone either. Richard had been right about that much. She had wanted him almost from the moment she first saw him arching his eyebrows at her on the ship's gangway.

But that was no reason to marry him.

'Listen to me, Elf,' he was saying, his eyes boring into hers, and his hands gripping her shoulders.

'I am listening. I haven't much choice.'

He took a quick breath, and she had a feeling that the imperturbable Mr Laslo was on the brink of losing his cool.

'True. You haven't. The point is...' He paused as if he were searching for the right words, then shrugged impatiently. 'The point is, I believe we'd suit each other, Elf. I'll admit I haven't thought much about the future since Felicity, but it's time I did. I've been thinking about it today.

'That's nice,' said Elf bitterly. 'Why?'

Unconsciously his grip on her shoulders tightened. 'I suppose because I was also thinking of the past. Our anniversary was one day out of the year that Felicity and I made a point of spending together.' He spoke without inflexion, as if it didn't matter.

'I'm sorry,' said Elf, who knew it did. When he didn't respond, she asked wearily, 'Why now, Richard? Why did you ask me to marry you today? Of all days?'

'Why not today? It seems—an appropriate time to make a new beginning. Felicity was never possessive. She'd understand and approve.'

'Oh. And did you imagine *I'd* approve?'

'You, my dear Elf, are alone in the world without even a job to fall back on. If you want to start a business, I've no objection to a wife who can stand on her own feet. I'd even be willing to back you. I think we understand each other, you and I, whether you're willing to admit it or not. And I can give you security, a home, all the material comforts——'

'And you don't love me.'

'Love?' Richard poured a wealth of contempt into the word. 'Dear lord, surely...' He stopped, and all at once his voice changed, became brisk and efficient. 'Never mind. As you've just assured me you don't love me either, that ought to simplify matters.'

Elf stared at him, and, without meaning to, she brushed her cheek over his hand. 'No,' she said. 'No, Richard, it doesn't. I don't want to marry for convenience. And I'm not at all sure I see why *you* do.'

The ghost of what might have been a smile touched the corner of his mouth and then vanished. 'Convenience?' he murmured. 'What makes you think you're convenient?'

She frowned, not understanding. 'Is that why you married Felicity?' she asked abruptly. 'Because you decided it was time to take a wife?'

A shadow passed over his face and she felt the fingers on her shoulders flex suddenly.

'No,' he rapped out. 'I married Felicity because I was young and quixotic and she was pregnant. The girl next door in trouble. I'd also managed to convince myself I loved her. I didn't know then that romantic love is nothing but a myth dreamed up by gangling adolescents.'

Elf winced. 'The—the baby was yours, then?' she finally managed to croak.

'No. Its father was heavily married—to somebody else who bred horses.'

Elf shook her head. 'Richard...' She lifted a hand to touch his face and then, realising what she was doing, dropped it back to her side. 'Richard, that was carrying good neighbourliness too far. Even for a gangling adolescent.' She tried to smile, but couldn't.

'I know,' he agreed, turning his head away briefly, so that Elf wasn't sure whether she had actually seen his lips tip up, or whether it was only her imagination. 'But in those days I was a confirmed romantic, convinced Felicity would see me as her knight in shining armour after I'd rescued her good name from the mud. When she lost the baby, though, it wasn't me she turned to, but her horses.'

Elf studied the minute lines fanning out from his eyes, noted the rigid way his shoulders were thrust back. 'So you *weren't*— happy,' she said slowly.

He shrugged. 'I spent over nine years of my life with Felicity. And I certainly wasn't happy that she died. Why? Does it matter?'

Elf nodded, not angry any more, but numb. 'Yes. I think it does.'

'Then yes. We were happy enough. Why not?'

Why not? thought Elf in confusion. Wasn't it obvious? Richard might have married in a fit of youthful quixotism because Felicity was pretty and pathetic and an old friend. But the love he bore her had apparently been tragically short-lived, snuffed out by the death of a child who wasn't his, and a wife who cared more for her horses than her husband. No wonder he thought love was a myth.

She shifted her back against the door, conscious of the pressure of his hands. Oh, yes, Richard's idea of marital happiness was extraordinarily different from her own. *He* had come to regard marriage as a useful business arrangement. He might once have fancied himself as a knight in shining armour, but somewhere along the way his knight errantry had taken a cynical turn for the worse.

'If that's all you wanted to tell me,' she said, with a weariness that went deeper than mere physical tiredness, 'I think we can consider this conversation closed. You married once for the wrong reasons. Surely you don't mean to make the same mistake again.'

'You're quite right.' His voice was clipped. 'I don't. I won't.'

'Then I don't see . . .' Something that might have been hope tugged at her heart before she could suppress it. 'Is there some other reason why you've come up with this crazy idea?' She didn't look at him.

An extra-large wave lurched beneath the ship and, overbalancing, Elf clutched at his arm. When she finally risked a glance at his face she saw that his nostrils had flared in that way that was so peculiarly daunting.

'You want another reason? All right, how about my mother wants grandchildren? She's not getting any younger, and her health isn't as robust as it was.'

Elf closed her eyes. 'Richard, you can't get married for the sake of your mother's health. People don't. And I can't get married for security and the prospect of a House and Garden home.'

'How very highly principled of you,' he taunted.

The sneer in his voice was the last straw. She stopped thinking and instinctively raised her hand to slap his face.

But before it could find its target he had caught her wrist. To her amazement he bit it gently and pushed it behind her back. Then he lowered his head. Elf just had time to gasp before his mouth came down hard over hers in a kiss that knocked the breath from her lungs. She felt his teeth graze her bottom lip as his fingers curled round the nape of her neck. When she tried to move her head, she found she couldn't. His tongue was in her mouth, velvet and intoxicating, and she didn't want to escape any more because, without having meant to, she was returning his kiss with a fierce hunger that locked them together in such passionate unity that she was left dazed, disorientated, not sure whether she was standing on her head or her heels.

As abruptly as he had kissed her, Richard let her go.

'That was just so you won't forget me,' he said, with a nonchalance that belied all the dreams that had momentarily spun through her head. 'Goodnight.'

Elf lifted her chin, refusing to let him see that she was hurting. A young man and a girl passing along the passage glanced curiously at the good-looking, tanned man and the petite, dark-haired woman, who a moment before had been kissing passionately, and now stood staring into each other's eyes as if they were total strangers.

Then Richard turned on his heel and strode away down the passage. Elf retrieved her key from the floor where it had fallen, and opened the door to her cabin. She wasn't conscious of the tears streaking down her face until one of them splashed on to her hand. She stared at it blankly. When the ship rolled unexpectedly she was caught off guard, and found herself slammed up against the wall.

That was when it hit her.

'What's the matter, dear? Anything I can do to help? You haven't been quite—quite yourself lately.' Elizabeth's gentle voice pierced the numbness that had anaesthetised

Elf's feelings for the past two days, and she turned from her blank concentration on the waves to see the older woman's gaze fastened on her in sympathetic concern.

'Haven't I?' asked Elf, relaxing her grip on the rail. 'I didn't realise . . . I guess I was just maintaining a low profile.'

Elizabeth smiled. 'Oh, it's certainly been low. You've been quiet as a dreamy little mouse. And you've worn only white or black clothes. You're not in mourning, I hope?'

'Oh, dear.' Elf smiled back guiltily. 'I'm sorry, I didn't mean to worry you. And no, I'm not in mourning, I promise.'

She was in a way, though, she thought, her mind returning, as it had so often, to that moment two nights ago when Richard had asked her to marry him. Yellow and shades of gold were the colours she normally chose, but she hadn't wanted to wear them since that night—because Richard had called her daffodil and said he liked her in yellow.

She remembered how he had left her with that casual, 'Goodnight,' and how she had bolted into her cabin and closed the door.

After that, with devastating clarity, and all the force of an axe splitting through wood, had come revelation.

She had done it again. Only this time it wasn't Harry or Tony. It was Richard Laslo, and the emotions she had felt in the past, and foolishly mistaken for love, were only the unfocused longings of a lonely young woman without any family to support her.

She knew that what she felt now was altogether different. She wanted to give to Richard, not take from him. She wanted to love him and live with him and make him happy. Yes, she thought despairingly—*and* to wake up beside him in the morning.

Oh, yes, she had done it again all right. With a vengeance. And her judgement, now that it mattered as it had never mattered before, had once again proved hopeless— fatally flawed and disastrous. Because although she had at last fallen in love with a man who was willing to marry her, he wanted her only as a convenience, because he'd sooner be married than not. Oh, he liked her well enough, of course. But he didn't love her, except, perhaps, in the same way he loved his antique brooches.

'Is it Richard?' Elizabeth's voice brought Elf back to her surroundings. There was a faint taste of salt on her lips.

'No, no, of course not,' she replied, turning up her collar as a sharp gust tugged at her hair. 'Richard has been charming. Very polite.'

It was true. Although Richard had made no further efforts to seek her out since the night of his proposal, when their paths happened to cross he had behaved towards her with perfect civility. The same civility he displayed towards every other passenger on the ship.

'Mmm.' Elizabeth eyed Elf doubtfully and pursed her lips so that folds of soft flesh gathered round her jawline. 'Sure you don't want to talk about it? Jerry's standing on his head in the gym, so I do have time.'

Elf laughed. 'No. Thank you. Really, I'm fine. And I have a golf lesson coming up soon.'

Elizabeth patted her arm. 'I know. You've been very occupied lately, haven't you? Movies, card games, lectures —— '

'Yes,' agreed Elf, hastily. 'I do like to keep busy.'

Keeping busy was the only way to stop herself from thinking. From dreaming about what might have been, if only things had been different...

But she couldn't tell Elizabeth that. This burden she would carry alone, as she had carried all other burdens since her parents died. She was used to coping by herself. There was no reason to break that pattern now.

The older woman seemed to understand, because she patted Elf's arm again and said that on second thoughts she'd better make sure Jerry was the right way up.

'He gets carried away,' she explained, 'and I'm not sure it's good for him. Besides, it's very hard to have a conversation with a pair of feet.'

Elf chuckled, and felt a vague stirring of envy. Jerry and Elizabeth were so contented, so at ease with each other—and still so obviously in love...

Only she mustn't think about love, she reminded herself. Love was for other people. The lucky ones. Not for cynics like Richard.

And for her—well, there was always golf.

The next day, the last before they were due to dock at Southampton, there was more golf.

Elf also played cards again, saw another movie, and in the evening watched the long-legged dancers for the last time.

It was much later, after she had fallen into a restless sleep, that she began to dream of Richard. He was standing on the bridge wearing a loincloth, and he seemed to be disguised as a witch doctor. Then the witch doctor wasn't Richard any more, he was the captain, and he was opening his mouth to issue orders in a flat, unhurried, but maddeningly persistent voice.

Elf woke up, feeling irritated and very sleepy. But the voice went on.

'I repeat, this is your captain speaking. There is a fire in the engine-room. It will be brought under control as quickly as possible. Stay in your cabins and keep all doors closed. There is no cause for alarm. Please remain where you are and await further instructions. I repeat, there is no cause for alarm.'

CHAPTER SEVEN

THE loudspeaker crackled and the message was repeated twice more.

Great, thought Elf. I wasn't alarmed, and I had no intention of opening doors until some disembodied voice woke me up and told me not to.

But she was wide awake now, and frightened. When people in authority insisted there was no need for alarm, experience had taught her there was every reason to worry.

'All very well for you, Captain,' she muttered at the unresponsive walls. *'You're* not sitting waiting to be cooked.'

She swung her feet out of bed and perched on the edge, listening. Further down the passage, doors slammed and a voice shouted. Then there was silence. No terrified screams, no ominous crackling of flames. Just the usual creaking, and an expectant, eerie absence of human noise.

Elf turned up the speaker. Not even static came over the air now. Only a sinister stillness.

She pulled at the hem of her nightdress, tightening it over her knees. It didn't help. Maybe she ought to get dressed. But if death was just around the corner—would anyone care what she was wearing?

The shower curtain slapped noisily in its stall, and all at once Elf felt an overwhelming longing to be with Richard. If only she had said yes that time he had asked her to marry him, she wouldn't be alone now. Alone and scared. She would be in his arms.

Biting the inside of her lip, and staring with grim concentration at the door, she tried, unsuccessfully, to keep her mind off the fire.

She wondered how her fellow passengers were coping. Were they taking the prospect of their imminent demise with equanimity? Jerry and Elizabeth might be. *They*, after all, would go together. Charles P. Waterbush was probably consuming a last snack. And Miranda? How would she be behaving? Most likely writing a letter of complaint, Elf thought bitterly. Tomorrow she would be telling them all that the *Sunshine Ship* would never have permitted a fire.

If there was a tomorrow.

She shivered.

The silence dragged on, and Elf felt as if she had been poised tensely on the edge of her bed for a century. Her body was stiffening into a cat-like arch, so she moved her head, wriggled her shoulders and lay down.

And immediately sat up again.

Something about the unnatural stillness had altered.

Suddenly the loudspeaker coughed. She had forgotten to turn it down, and the sound, blasting through the previous deathlike silence, made her jump so that her head banged against the wall. She winced, and adjusted the speaker to the point where she could distinguish words. The captain was speaking again.

The fire was out. Everything was under control. They could all go back to their beds.

'Thank God,' whispered Elf, releasing the breath she seemed to have been holding forever. Her first reaction was one of ecstatic relief. An instant later, relief was followed by an almost light-headed disbelief that things could possibly have returned to normal. Then she recollected that the captain had suggested going back to bed, and disbelief gave way to indignation.

'I *was* in bed,' she grumbled, glaring at the silent speaker. 'Fat chance I've got of sleeping now.'

Out in the passage she could hear doors opening, and voices shouting and laughing. One voice, louder than the others, was screaming hysterically. Elf had heard that particular screech before.

She had thrown off her nightdress and was beginning to fasten her black skirt when there was an imperative knock on the door.

'Who is it?' she called, hastily pulling on a blouse.

'Richard. Open up.'

Elf gasped. Earlier there had been no voice she would have given more to hear. Yet now she felt her hackles rising at his calm assumption that he had a right to demand instant admittance.

All the same, she let him in at once.

Without a word he stepped across the threshold and kicked the door shut. Elf eyed him warily as he propped himself against the wall and stood staring at her, his arms folded sternly on his chest.

'Are you all right?' he demanded, after a few seconds which Elf spent gazing at the taut sinews of his neck. There was a grimness, a tension in his voice that she had never heard there before.

'Yes, I'm fine,' she said, unbearably aware of the scent of him, of his closeness here in her small cabin.

She raised her eyes then, looking for tell-tale signs of soot or scorched skin. But all she saw was the immaculate white jacket he had worn at dinner, and above it the tanned but quite unroasted face of the man she loved. The face she had so often felt an unladylike urge to scratch—and kiss, and run her fingers over. And do anything to that would wipe that mocking smile off his lips. Only he wasn't smiling now. His expression was grim, yet strangely seductive. And the eyes that searched her face were probing and pos-sessive, but not laughing.

'Yes, I see you *are* all right,' he said when his careful scrutiny was beginning to cause a melting below her knees.

She nodded. 'Of course I am. And why should that matter to you?'

Richard curved his hands over her upper arms, his gaze travelling with cool appraisal over her unbuttoned blouse, and the skirt which still hung precariously low on her hips.

'Do I detect a note of sarcasm?' he asked. 'It doesn't become you. And why wouldn't I be concerned about the welfare of my old partner in crime?'

Oh. So that was all his presence meant. Unconsciously, Elf let her shoulders droop.

'You haven't been to bed,' she said inanely, because there didn't seem anything else to say.

Richard raised his impressive eyebrows. 'And you, apparently, sleep with your clothes on. Or half on. You're full of surprises, aren't you?'

'No. Yes. I don't sleep with my clothes on.' Elf fumbled nervously with a button. 'Your hair's brushed, and your tie's on straight and—and you look so clean and tidy, so...' She stopped, realising too late that in her relief that he was unharmed, and her confusion over her half-dressed appearance, she was talking nonsense—as well as giving too much away.

'Well, now,' drawled Richard, moving his hands slowly down her arms. 'I've been accused of a number of things in my life, but never of being clean and tidy. Elf, my sweet, I believe our little emergency has addled your brain.'

'My feather-brain?' suggested Elf, beginning to recover her composure.

There was a warning glint in her eye which wasn't lost on Richard as he curled long fingers round her wrists and parted his lips in a grin that was pure provocation. 'Mmm. Turkey down, I imagine. Or maybe ostrich.'

'Oh!' Elf didn't know whether she wanted to laugh or slap him. In the end, surprising herself, she aimed a half-hearted kick at his shins. And missed.

Richard, with an oath, pinned both her wrists behind her back. Instantly she was trapped against him with her forehead touching the buttons of his shirt. She could smell the warm, virile scent of his aftershave.

'Try that again and I'll break your arm,' he said softly.

Elf looked up quickly, half believing him, but the taunting green eyes that met hers were bright with amused satisfaction.

'I think you were less obnoxious in the days when you used to pull my hair for cheeking you,' she told him crossly, annoyed with herself for being taken in by his threat.

'I'll pull it again if you like,' he offered. One of his hands still held her wrists. The other was twisted in her curls. She could feel his fingers brushing her scalp.

Their eyes met again, hers doubtful, his gleaming with intent, and, as she stood motionless, slowly, deliciously, his lips closed over hers.

She felt his tongue slide between her teeth as he released her wrists and slipped his arm round her waist. Just for a moment, she resisted. Then, at the touch of his lips, the strain of the past hour seemed to burst inside her like a fragile bubble. All memory of fear was washed away, and she returned his embrace with a sense that this, at last, was the place where she was meant to be. Felicity, his passionless marriage, his proposal of another marriage—of convenience this time—none of it mattered any more.

Richard shifted his hips, played his fingers up and down her spine, and when her unbuttoned skirt dropped softly on to the floor neither of them paid any attention.

At first his kiss was exploratory, cool and tasting, but after a few seconds it became insistent, passionately demanding and probing, as she moulded her body to his and gave herself up to the warmth of his caress. His hands slid down, lifting her hips against his thighs, and, without knowing she was doing it, Elf moaned softly.

At once, and to her total confusion, he released her. She staggered back. The cabin seemed to revolve around her head, and, when it finally came back into focus, she saw that his green eyes were fixed on her with an almost frightening intensity.

She stared at him, speechless, as gradually his breathing slowed, and he ran a hand through his hair. 'If you keep kissing me like that, Makepeace,' he said, glancing at the rumpled skirt by her feet, 'and if you persist in flaunting yourself half naked —— '

Elf gasped. 'I'm not half naked,' she protested, pulling futilely at the bottom of her blouse.

Richard stopped looking intense and gave her a sardonic smile. 'No? I suppose if you

count those indecently brief yellow panties...'
He paused. 'On second thoughts, I must be
going out of my mind. Let's *not* count them.'

Elf held her breath as he took a purposeful
step towards her. He was loosening his tie as
he advanced and he had the air of a man who
had made up his mind what he wanted and
intended to have it. And marriage was no
longer the issue...

She moistened her lips, gulped, began to
raise her arms—not sure, in that moment, if
she meant to welcome his advance or repulse
him.

She never found out, because, just as his
firm hands closed around her scantily clad
hips, something thudded against the door
behind them. It sounded very much like a
body hitting wood, and was followed by a
funny, burbling groan.

Richard jerked his head back and let his
arms drop.

Outside the cabin, the shouting which had
been going on ever since the end of the
emergency roared to a crescendo and ceased
abruptly. Elf opened her mouth to speak, but,
above the sudden silence, a shrill voice started
to scream.

'Help! The ship's sinking. Help me up. Ooh, I've sprained my ankle. Save me. I don't want to die. Women and children first...'

It was a performance worthy of Bernhardt—and Elf had a feeling the timing was by no means an accident. Not if Miranda had seen Richard enter her cabin.

Richard looked at Elf and shrugged. 'Do we ignore it?' he asked.

Elf, transfixed by the question in his eyes, understood that a great deal depended on her answer. She brushed a hand over her forehead. 'I—I...' she began.

'Yes?' Cool, a little harsh, not as if it really mattered.

And it was too soon. She felt threatened, intimidated by this formidable man she had grown to love much too quickly. This man who didn't need her as she needed him.

'No, we don't ignore it,' she said quietly. 'Maybe there really is something wrong.' She stared at the floor, all of a sudden embarrassed to meet his eyes.

A small bleak smile touched his mouth, and he gave her a mocking little bow. 'Very well, milady. In that case, mission postponed. Indefinitely.' He bent down to pick up her skirt and, handing it to her, said briskly, 'Put this on.'

Before she could react, he had disappeared into the passageway and was snapping the door shut behind him.

Miranda's screams grew louder.

Elf, her eyes blank, began to pull on her skirt. 'Heaven help me,' she whispered.

If Miranda had not intervened, would she have let Richard make love to her? Would he have tried? And if he came back, what then? She moved into the bathroom, gripped the edge of the basin and stared at her face in the mirror. Her eyes were smudged and dark, but her skin shone with a warm pink glow that had nothing to do with the *Supership's* heating system. She drew in her breath as the suspicion came to her that if Richard did come back she might not have the will to resist him.

'And you don't even want to resist him,' she said accusingly to the face in the mirror.

'Yes, I do.' The words were coming from her own reflection. 'Of course I do. Anyway, he won't come back. He said "mission postponed. Indefinitely". Now stop being such a fool, Elf Makepeace, and find out what's happening out there.'

Taking her own advice, Elf stepped into the passage just in time to hear the resounding slap of flesh meeting flesh. It was followed by a gulping little moan. Then she saw that the now silent group of celebrants was gathered around the trembling form of Miranda, who was crouched against the wall with a hand pressed up to her face. When she lowered it, one cheek was slashed a bright, livid red. Her eyes, round and disbelieving, were fixed on Richard, who was standing with a hand out-stretched to help her up.

'He hit me,' whispered Miranda, pointing.

Elf looked round. Charles P. Waterbush, dressed in a vast crimson silk bathrobe, was staring, mouth agape, at his own hand.

'Didn't mean to,' he muttered. 'Just passing on my way to the night kitchen. Terrible noise. Had to stop it ——'

'Don't worry about it,' Richard inter-rupted, pulling Miranda on to her feet. 'Somebody had to. She was hysterical.'

Miranda smiled at him tremulously and blinked her limpid blue eyes. 'Dear Richard. I know *you* wouldn't have hit me. I was so scared, and that man...' She frowned at Charles and shuddered daintily. 'Oh, I don't

know what I'd have done, Richard, if you
hadn't come——'

'Gone on making that nauseating noise, I
expect,' muttered Elf.

Richard glanced sideways, and she thought
she read wry agreement in his eyes before he
turned back to Miranda.

'The fire's out, the ship's not sinking, and
you're quite all right now,' he assured her
briskly.

'Well, almost.' She giggled. 'Now that
you're here. And tomorrow we'll all be safely
in England. You and I must meet in London,
mustn't we, Richard?' She placed a hand on
his arm and smiled winsomely.

Elf didn't hear Richard's reply, because she
had decided to be sick instead. Any more of
Miranda's saccharine soft soap and she
wouldn't be responsible for her actions.
Taking a deep breath, she stepped quietly
back into her cabin and closed the door.

A few minutes later she thought she heard
another high-pitched giggle, followed by
Richard's deep, masculine tones. After that
the noise of celebration started up again and
clamoured for a while before drifting away
down the passage.

Then there was only the sound of the sea, and the persistent creaking of the ship in the night.

Elf went back to bed, but not to sleep. In her mind she kept reliving those fraught seconds before Miranda had shattered what might have been with her practised screams. If that hadn't happened, *would* she have let Richard love her? And did he really care about her at all? He had come to her because he felt a dutiful obligation to a childhood friend. Only he hadn't behaved like a friend...

A long time later, when she was almost asleep, Elf thought she heard a knock on her door. She listened, but the noise was not repeated and she decided it must have been rats. She glanced dubiously over the edge of her bed. No, modern ships weren't supposed to carry rats, were they? She must have been dreaming. Rolling on to her side, she squeezed her eyes resolutely shut.

Elf hurried to breakfast with a feeling of anticipation. She hadn't really expected Richard to return to her last night, because she had suspected all along that his shining armour had never been totally discarded. She wasn't surprised that latent gentlemanly scruples had got the better of him once immediate temptation was removed. But their relationship had shifted on to a different plane some time during the small hours of the morning, and she *had* hoped... Anyway today held a promise—a promise and a dream that hadn't been there before. She felt different today. She wasn't sure why, but she did.

Richard was not at the table. Jerry and Elizabeth were, and Charles P. Waterbush was already ploughing his way through croissants and strawberry jam as he awaited the arrival of eggs, bacon, pancakes and two helpings of hash brown potatoes.

Just as Elf sat down, Miranda sauntered up to join them. She was dressed in a flamboyant emerald-green suit which clung to every curve of her luscious body. It totally eclipsed Elf's fitted trousers and jacket. But the beauty's rose-bud smile was forced, and she cast a look of loathing at the top of Charles P's bent head. She showed no sign of weariness after her Oscar-winning performance of the night before.

'Hasn't it been a wonderful voyage?' she gurgled. 'So special.'

Elf choked into her coffee, and Miranda's gracious smile became even more forced. 'It's not the *Sunshine Ship*, of course,' she added hastily, 'but there *have* been compensations. I'm sure you'll find someone too some day, Elf. A nice, comfortable little man with a small shop. That ought to suit you very well.'

Elf concentrated on her toast and refused to rise to the other woman's childish provocation. Was Miranda suggesting that she had succeeded in scoring a *coup*? Namely, a not particularly nice but devastatingly sexy man with a very *large* shop? If so, Elf didn't believe it for a moment. But she did wish Richard would come.

She put down her napkin and announced that she was going on deck to catch her first glimpse of England.

Elizabeth nodded. 'It will be nice to see land again, won't it?'

'Yes, it will.' Elf rose to her feet and strolled out of the dining-room as if she hadn't a care in the world—or a disgracefully immature urge to punch a certain redhead's patrician nose.

Richard wasn't on deck. Or, if he was, she couldn't find him. Perhaps he was still packing, although luggage was already beginning to pile up by the gangway entrance.

After searching the lounge, the bars, the gym and the swimming-pool with no success, she decided to telephone his cabin.

The line was busy.

Relieved, Elf returned to the upper deck. Richard was on the phone, that was all. Whatever the future might hold, it was unthinkable that he would leave the *Supership* without troubling to say goodbye to her. Not that he *could* leave just yet. They wouldn't dock for several more hours, and even Richard didn't have wings.

Smiling at her own foolishness, she leaned over the ship's rail between an excited little girl who kept jumping up and down and squealing, and a taciturn old man who was smoking a particularly foul cigar.

Across a narrow stretch of sunlit sea she watched the patchwork coast of England pass them by. With its neat, hedged-in fields, it reminded her of her mother's favourite quilt. The little girl squealed again, and Elf smiled wistfully. She felt a little like squealing herself, but for a different reason.

Here she was at last, catching her first glimpse of her mother's native land, and all she could think of was the cool arch of Richard Laslo's eyebrows. Where on earth was he? Surely he wasn't avoiding her? Or could his suggestion that they ignore Miranda's antics last night have been his final offer? With marriage no longer an option, had he decided to substitute raw sex? Take it or leave it, now or never sex.

Elf closed her eyes. Yes. That could be it. In which case she had made the right decision.

Why, then, she wondered anxiously, as she stared at a distant flock of sheep, did it feel so wrong?

A fresh cloud of cigar smoke blew into her face, and she went downstairs to telephone Richard's cabin again.

This time there was no answer.

When she returned to the upper deck, the ship had already docked, and she found Jerry and Elizabeth standing by the rail with Charles, who was munching on an orange with pensive gloom.

'They're making us disembark before lunch,' he announced morosely.

'Yes,' agreed Elf. 'In about an hour, I think.'

Charles gave a rumbling kind of groan, which made Jerry grin. Elf had no trouble keeping her face straight. She couldn't have laughed if she'd tried.

'What's the matter, dear?' asked Elizabeth, always perceptive.

Elf was about to say nothing was, when the older woman added softly, 'It's not Richard, is it?'

'Richard?' Elf smiled blankly. 'What about him?'

Jerry cleared his throat, glanced at Elizabeth, then stared at the grey clouds gathering in the sky. Finally he said, 'You do know, don't you, that he's left the ship?'

CHAPTER EIGHT

ELF'S heart lurched so hard that it almost hurt. 'Left the ship?' she repeated stupidly.

Jerry nodded, his impish face creased apologetically, as if he felt responsible for her pain. 'Yes, as soon as we docked. He was able to arrange special clearance.'

'Oh,' whispered Elf. 'I didn't know. He—he didn't say...'

'He probably didn't have time,' Jerry assured her quickly. '*We* only found out because he happened to pass us on his way to the gangway. Apparently there's been a major break-in at Laslo's, and a lot of priceless jewellery was stolen. His office contacted him last night—some time after the fire, I think he said. He only spoke to us for a moment.' The small man grinned, and Elf knew he was trying to cheer her up. 'From the look on young Richard's face, I wouldn't want to be in the thieves' shoes if he gets his hands on them.'

'No,' agreed Elf in a small voice. 'Neither would I.'

Richard had a passion for his cold but colourful gems—a passion that he'd as good as admitted he wasn't capable of feeling for a mere woman. He wouldn't take kindly to being robbed.

'He—he didn't leave a message or anything, did he?' Elf asked, knowing he hadn't, and hating herself for betraying how much she cared.

'I'm sure he would have,' said Elizabeth kindly, 'but I expect it slipped his mind in all the confusion. He mentioned he'd been on the phone half the night.'

'Yes,' said Elf. 'Of course. It doesn't matter.'

But they all knew it did matter, even Charles, who began searching his pockets for food which he might have overlooked. When he came up, glumly, with half a peanut and two peppermints, he offered Elf one.

She almost burst into tears.

For a while the four of them stood about making desultory conversation, and when that began to wear thin they all developed urgent business elsewhere. Goodbyes, quick and a little sad, were exchanged, and they went their separate ways anxious to avoid prolonged farewells.

Elf stood by the rail blowing her nose. This was the end, then. She wouldn't even get to say goodbye. She rubbed her eyes, and stared glassily at a frantically embracing couple. Richard wasn't on board. There was no point in searching any further.

A couple of hours later she stood alone on the dock at Southampton.

The sun which had dappled the coast had given way to a misty wet drizzle.

'It figures,' she muttered to a startled customs officer. 'All my life I've dreamed of this moment, and, now that I'm here, it's raining.'

But in her heart she knew that rain wasn't her problem, and that the dream had been shattered hours before. Eyes glazed and fixed straight ahead, she trudged past a squawking Miranda, who was engaged in a dispute over baggage with a large lady sporting a bun, and splashed her way over to the boat train.

She felt bereft, angry, abandoned—and filled with a deeper regret than any she had known in her life.

Richard had given up on her. She had rejected him last night because loving him wouldn't give her everything she needed. And he had taken her rejection at face value and not cared enough to restake his claim. So she had lost him. Lost, perhaps, something she had never truly had. None the less, it was more than Tony had offered. More than she had now. Without Richard there was no one to give her life a dimension that stretched beyond earning a living and keeping in touch with her friends. No one to make her angry, to make her sad, to make her laugh. To love.

Elf shifted her shoulders against the hard train seat and stared, without really seeing him, at a man with a bristling moustache.

She would be lonely in the years that lay ahead. Unbearably so. But she had been lonely before and survived. She would again. What choice had she?

Seeing her defiant glare, and thinking it was directed at him, the man with the moustache coughed uncomfortably and disappeared behind his paper.

'Get up, get up,' a raucous voice commanded.

Elf blinked her eyes open, gaped at neon-pink wallpaper and a toy tiger perched on a shelf, and pushed herself up on her pillows.

'Get up,' the voice repeated.

'I am up,' muttered Elf. 'Who do you...?' Oh. Of course.

Last night the tourist office had found her a small boarding-house near Sloane Square called the Bonavista. Not that there was much vista about it, she remembered. Only a few skinny trees which had survived their planting like neglected street urchins, beside a row of skinny brick houses. Inside the Bonavista, faded antique furniture sagged under tatty lace covers, and every flat surface groaned beneath a multitude of knick-knacks. In the upstairs hall, a minah bird called Spinach held court from a gold-painted cage.

'Get up,' he shouted again.

Useful, thought Elf wryly. With a wake-up call like that, it was a safe bet no guest was ever late for breakfast.

Which was lucky for her, she decided an hour and a half later when she alighted from the Underground on to rain-slicked pavements near the Tower of London. There was no sense spending her first full day in England lolling in bed.

She shoved to the back of her mind the wayward thought that, in circumstances that now would never happen, bed would be anything but a waste. She knew she had lost that hope forever when she had allowed Miranda's dramatics to achieve their aim.

Doggedly she made her way along the street to where she could see the Tower's solid battlements pointing up at the sky.

By the time she emerged again, sated with history and crowds, but feeling that the past, with its beheadings and battles, had moved uncannily close, the sun was beaming weakly from behind a cloud.

Elf stared at the famous outline of Tower Bridge traced darkly against the skyline, and hoped it wasn't going to start to rain again. She didn't need weather to match her mood, which was gloomy enough as it was. What she did need, she supposed, was something to take home to her friend Sandra. Sandra collected tacky souvenirs, and there was a souvenir shop just across the road.

She edged her way through the narrow doorway, and shuffled past the inevitable collection of miniature Towers, overpriced china, and cheap pictorial ashtrays. But it wasn't the usual bric-a-brac that caught her eye. Instead her gaze was drawn irresistibly to a discreet display of lace-trimmed tartan panties. She blinked doubtfully. Not Sandra's style really, but...

Elf poked at the panties, imagining the expression on her friend's face when she was presented with a pair of Hunting Red Robinson underpants.

The temptation was overwhelming. Elf reached for her purse.

'A very wise purchase,' a cool voice murmured in her ear. 'You'll be irresistible in those, daffodil. I can hardly wait.'

Elf whirled, the red panties falling from her fingers to drape themselves over a statuette of Queen Victoria.

'Richard!' she gasped. 'Why in the world...?' Her voice trailed off, and she put a hand up to cover her eyes. They were filling with tears. Tears she didn't want him to see. She swallowed hard, and in a moment was able to look at him again. 'You won't get a chance to resist anything,' she told him huskily. 'So you needn't bother about waiting.'

Joy, overwhelming and undeniable, had at first threatened to drown out every other emotion. But gradually, as a complacent smile lifted the corner of his mouth, that joy was being tempered by a quite unreasonable confusion at being caught with the tartan panties.

'Won't I?' drawled Richard. 'Don't count on it.' He allowed his gaze to run lazily over her small figure in smart black trousers and yellow blouse. 'Do you know, Elf Makepeace, for a few seconds there you actually looked quite pleased to see me? But for now, at least, I believe I'll settle for lunch instead.'

'Instead of what?' asked Elf, her heart still doing cartwheels as she took in the intimidating dark blue suit which accentuated his tan and hinted tantalisingly at the powerful body concealed beneath its businesslike lines.

'From my point of view, instead of admiring an overdressed Elf in lace-trimmed tartan panties which will need to be speedily removed,' he said briskly.

Elf's heart returned to its rightful place as she subdued an unladylike urge to stick her tongue out. 'The panties are for my friend Sandra, not for me,' she informed him loftily.

Richard shrugged. 'How disappointing.'
Then, as she moved towards the cash register,
he added with a wicked leer, 'When can I meet
your friend Sandra?'

Without stopping to think, Elf seized the
controversial underwear, which was hanging
from the royal ear, and aimed it smartly at
his head.

He stepped equally smartly aside, and her
missile scored a bullseye on a row of pictorial
brass ashtrays.

'Here, that's enough of that,' shouted an
irate voice, as the owner of the shop bustled
agggressively from behind his counter.

'I'm so sorry,' mumbled Elf, turning almost
as red as the panties. 'I don't think I broke
anything, though.'

'No, you didn't. You're a damn poor shot,
Miss Makepeace.' Richard's mocking remark
came to her from the safety of the doorway.

Elf considered jamming the panties over his
patronising, supercilious head, but thought
better of it when the owner took a step in her
direction.

'Er—I really am sorry,' she mumbled
again, beating a hasty retreat to the door.

Richard was now lounging against the outside wall with his hands in the pockets of his trousers. His gleaming white shirt stretched enticingly across the breadth of his chest.

Damn it, he's got no right to be so sexy, fumed Elf, as she hurried past him into the street.

Richard smiled down at her, green eyes glittering. 'That should teach you,' he remarked, placing long fingers at the back of her neck.

'No, it shouldn't. Teach me what?' asked Elf, pulling her head away, and wishing she didn't feel she had to. She liked the cool touch of his hand against her skin.

'To behave like a lady,' he replied, assuming an old-fashioned expression which made her want to hit him. Hard. She glowered, and at once he began to whistle a menacing little tune between his teeth. Elf was reminded that it had never been a good idea to arouse Richard's retaliatory instincts.

'Lunch, I think,' he murmured, taking her firmly by the arm. 'Maybe food will improve your disposition.'

'I don't want lunch,' said Elf, who was starving.

'Well, I do, and I don't propose to eat it alone.' He began to march her down the street.

Elf removed her elbow from his grasp and stepped backwards.

Immediately he looped his long arm around her waist. 'You're not going anywhere,' he said curtly.

His breath lifted the curls above her ear, and Elf felt her stomach lurch lustfully. He was right. She wasn't going anywhere. Not unless he came too. There was no point in deluding herself. He was here, beside her where he seemed to belong, and what she wanted, more than anything she had ever wanted before, was this man. This sensation of burning, stomach-churning excitement was something she had never even come close to, and, however much her head told her she ought to scream for help from the nearest passer-by, her heart kept her close at Richard's side. So did his hand as he dropped it loosely down over her hip.

She glanced at him almost shyly, and then pulled herself up straight. Something about his angular profile reminded her of the way

he had looked when he'd told her love was
only for gangling adolescents.

Right. Lunch, not lust, would have to be
the order of the day.

'Is something the matter?' asked Richard,
as she stepped on his toe.

'No, nothing,' she replied firmly.

'Good,' he said, leading her across a
cobbled courtyard at the back of which was
parked a large white car. 'I'd hate to think my
toe had been reduced to chipsteak for any
particular reason.'

'I'm sorry,' said Elf, coming to a stop. 'Did
I hurt you?'

'No. Disappointed?'

Elf sighed. 'Of course not. Why should I
be?'

'I've no idea. But I have a strong impression that I'm on your hit list today.'

'I don't have a hit list.'

'Don't you?'

She stared at him. His nostrils were flared
slightly, and she had the definite feeling that
he was trying to provoke her into admitting
something she'd very likely regret.

'No, I don't,' she replied shortly, as he
opened the door of the car and helped her in.

She took in the luxurious black upholstery and expensive fittings. 'Richard, is this yours?'

'Is what mine?'

'This car. It's a Rolls.'

'I know. And yes, it is mine.'

'Oh.' She subsided into the cushions, deciding a little guiltily that she could easily become used to this style of living.

Richard threaded his way, with dexterity and one hand, through traffic which Elf, used to wider streets and driving on the right-hand side of the road, found hair-raising. But, within what seemed to her a very short space of time, they were in Mayfair, and the Rolls was pulling up near a world-famous and very exclusive hotel whose impressive portals she had never expected to cross.

'But we can't—I'm not dressed...' Elf stumbled over her words as Richard took her arm and led her towards a uniformed doorman who was opening the door for them with a disdainful expression which she was sure was directed at her.

'Of course you're dressed,' said Richard impatiently. 'Even I would draw the line at

taking a naked woman to lunch in broad day-
light. Besides, you look very presentable.'

Elf gaped at him. That, she supposed,
was a compliment—not something Richard
handed out lightly. All the same, trousers and
a bright yellow blouse...

'Yes, but...' She tried to pull away from
him.

Richard, with a sigh of exasperation, said,
'Elf. Shut up. You're with me.'

As if that was the end of the matter, she
thought dazedly. Looking up at the doorman,
who bowed his head as they passed, she
realised with a start that it *was* the end.
Richard Laslo was no longer the high-spirited
boy she had once known, but a man of power
and substance whose name would be recognised in all sorts of far-flung corners of the
globe. And if he chose to escort a small
woman dressed in trousers and a blouse, no
one would so much as raise an eyebrow.

Still feeling dazed, Elf followed Richard
across the high-ceilinged lobby into the sort
of dining-room she had read of in Regency
novels, but hadn't imagined actually existed.
Her first impression was of quiet elegance and

total discretion, her second of understated luxury.

'Your usual table, sir?' enquired the attentive head waiter, who had materialised the moment they stepped through the doors.

Richard nodded, and they were shown to a table in an alcove set comfortably away from the other diners. Elf sat down feeling a little over-awed and very hungry. As well as curious.

'Richard, why—how did you happen to find me?' she asked. 'You can't have followed me——'

'Why can't I?'

'Well, because—because you didn't even bother to say goodbye. So why would you want to come after me?'

Richard picked up the wine list, gave it a perfunctory glance, and nodded to their waiter, who nodded back and disappeared through an oak-panelled doorway.

When they were alone again, Richard said, 'The truth is I *didn't* want to come after you. Oh, I admit I once thought we might suit each other quite well. But *you* didn't, and I changed my mind. A clean break seemed the obvious solution.'

'For you or for me?'

He shrugged. 'For both of us. I saw no point in continuing to press my suit with a woman who, in many ways, is still the stubborn little girl I used to know, and who, if I'm not mistaken, is more than a little afraid of me.'

The waiter returned to open the wine bottle and take their orders, giving Elf time to recover her composure. She didn't want Richard to see that his dismissive words were hurting her far beyond reason. She'd been so happy to see him again, but it seemed his unexpected reappearance in her life had nothing to do with a sudden realisation that he needed her.

'Not afraid,' she said, not looking at him, because if she did she wouldn't be able to keep her voice under control. 'Just confused.'

'Mmm. That did occur to me later. Which was why, when Jerry Bridger got in touch with me and told me I was a heartless swine for running out on you, I decided I'd better give you another chance.' He picked up his glass and said lightly, 'Here's to second chances.'

Elf gasped. 'Give *me* another... Of all the arrogant ── '

He smiled. 'Yes, my dear. You've told me that before.'

Elf picked up her knife and began to put too much butter on a roll. 'I'm not your dear,' she said finally, at a loss for a more effective come-back, and feeling as winded as if he'd just kicked her.

'I'm inclined to agree,' he said drily.

The soup arrived then, a rich creamy asparagus that went down as smoothly as butter. Elf consumed it silently, knowing that, if she uttered even one word, it was likely to be one word too many. Besides, she had a better chance of pinning Richard down on a full stomach.

'I do like a lady with an appetite,' he observed, watching the speed at which her soup disappeared.

Elf took another sip. 'Do you? I thought you told me I wasn't a lady.'

'Wishful thinking, I expect.'

Elf sighed. He wasn't going to make anything easy for her, and she began to wish she hadn't come here after all. A small bar, where no one would care much if she dumped the soup on his head, would have much better suited her inclinations.

The moment the thought crossed her mind, it came to her that her soup seemed to have rather less taste than before.

'I want to know how you found me, and *why* you found me,' she said, taking the bull by the horns, and deciding to ignore all provocation. 'You still haven't bothered to explain.'

Richard leaned back in his chair. He seemed to be looking at something behind her head. 'Would you rather I hadn't found you?' he asked.

'No, of course not. It's lucky for me you showed up.'

'Why's that?' He stopped looking over her and looked at her.

'I got a free lunch, didn't I?' She couldn't resist needling him after all.

Richard waited until the soup bowls had been cleared away and replaced by a fish course. Then he said, in a voice that wasn't quite steady, 'You, Elfriede Makepeace, are an unprincipled little gold-digger. Are you trying to tell me I won the doubtful pleasure of your company not with my devastating charm, but with a rather pleasant wine, and dead halibut?'

'Mm,' she said untruthfully. 'More or less. But don't worry about it—your ego can use some deflating.'

'No doubt,' he agreed, eyes narrowing in a contemplative way she didn't trust.

Elf finished the last of her halibut a little too fast, took a sip of her wine and said briskly, before he could distract her again, 'Richard?'

'Mm-hm?'

'*Why* did you come looking for me? If you did.'

Richard picked up his glass, drank, then put it down again very deliberately. She felt as if the clear beam of his eyes had her impaled like a butterfly on a board.

'I didn't,' he said. 'Having more pressing business to attend to, I had my usual agency track you down.'

'Oh.' Elf digested that. 'Why, then?'

'As I've already told you, Jerry Bridger called me. He seemed to think that being deprived of my stimulating company might drive you into a decline.'

'Huh. Don't flatter yourself,' scoffed Elf. She stared down at the table for a while, then sighed heavily. 'I guess Jerry meant well, though. Did he really call you a swine?'

'He did.'

'And that bothered you?' She didn't believe it.

'No. But it did make me think that if by chance he was right about you I owed myself the pleasure of observing the phenomenon for myself.' His smile was a bare movement of the lips.

Not promising, thought Elf, trying to feel indignant, and finding that all she really felt was hopeless. Richard didn't care about her. He just wanted her to regret turning him down.

She lifted her head in time to see him flex his shoulders, and something clutched at her stomach. Lust again, she thought disgustedly. When the feeling inside her began to turn into an actual pain, she decided desire was an overrated emotion.

'Why waste your time?' she asked irritably, as a rush of warmth flowed to her skin, and the odd sensation in her stomach eased slightly. 'You weren't interested in observing me on the ship once I'd convinced you I didn't want to marry you. Until the night of the fire, that is. And even after that you—you just left.'

Richard smiled without a trace of warmth. 'Are you telling me that distressed you? How satisfactory. I rather thought a little ignoring would do you good. And, in case it's slipped your mind, after the fire I had the small matter of a robbery to attend to.'

'Which probably did *you* good,' Elf retorted.

'Hmm.' He shot her a look she couldn't interpret. 'Perhaps it did.'

Now what did he mean by that? she wondered. That he'd been glad of the excuse to leave the ship? 'Did you get your stolen jewellery back?' she asked, not caring much.

'Yes, most of it. Criminals aren't usually too bright. This lot left a trail as easy to trace as bad cheese. Now why don't you tell me what's really on your mind?'

'Oh. You —— ' Elf stabbed her finger into a drop of wine on the table and dug her teeth into her lip.

'Yes?'

She took a deep breath. Richard was being his usual maddening self. Cool, lightly mocking and imperturbable. And her head

was beginning to feel as odd as her stomach.
All the same, her heart would never give her
any peace until she knew...

'After the fire,' she said, forcing herself to
sound indifferent. 'After the fire, when you
went off with Miranda —— '

'I did not go off with Miranda,' Richard
interrupted. 'And don't make us sound like a
pair of decomposing kippers. I *did* escort her
to her cabin. If I hadn't, I'm afraid poor
Charles P. Waterbush would never have made
it through the night.'

'What are you talking about?'

'Charles P. Waterbush. Miranda had him
convinced he'd injured her for life. I had to
prove to him that she was in good working
order, able to walk and, more importantly, to
eat. But the only way I could do that was by
taking her arm and accompanying her to her
destination.'

'Bed.'

'Precisely. So I deposited her outside her
door and suggested she could do with some
sleep.'

'Gallant of you,' said Elf drily. 'And not
at all what she hoped for.'

'Probably not. Nevertheless, I went back to my cabin—just in time to receive the news of the break-in. When I realised I was unlikely to have time in the morning, I decided I'd better say goodbye to you at once.'

'Goodbye?'

'That's right. What else did you think I had in mind?'

He looked so aloof now, so condescending, that Elf didn't think he'd had anything in mind. She shook her head. 'Nothing.'

'Exactly. By that time sanity was well and truly restored. Just as well, in view of the fact that when I knocked on your door you didn't answer.' He tipped his head back, eyelids drooping lazily.

So he had come back. Elf hiccuped, as once again something grabbed at her insides. Rallying quickly, she managed to mutter, 'Sorry. At the time I thought you were rats.' She reached for her glass, misjudged the distance and slammed her hand on the table.

Richard fixed an austere eye on her damaged knuckles. 'If you weren't sufficiently bruised already, I'd be inclined to add a few more for that remark.'

'No, you wouldn't,' said Elf, with an assurance that took her by surprise. 'You're not like that.'

'Don't be too sure of that. You try me severely at times, Makepeace.'

Richard's tone was soft, drawling and faintly suggestive, and, if Elf hadn't discovered that her head was beginning to feel very peculiar, she might have considered walking out. As it was, when she raised her hand to press it to her throbbing temples her mind veered off in quite another direction, and she remembered her original grievance.

'You never *did* say goodbye,' she grumbled, taking a small spoonful of the sorbet the waiter had just placed in front of her.

Richard rested his forearms on the table and bent towards her. Smiling. It wasn't a smile calculated to ease her mind. 'I didn't, did I? But keep scowling at me like that, Elfriede, and I certainly will say goodbye. Permanently. Is that what you want?'

'It's what you want, isn't it?' said Elf, still scowling.

She saw his lips thin forbiddingly. 'I certainly thought it was. I'm beginning to think so again.'

Elf tried to glare at him, and discovered that he had mysteriously acquired two heads. 'I don't see why...' she began, then closed her eyes very quickly.

'You don't see why I don't behave as you have evidently decided I ought to? Because, my sweet, I have not yet succeeded in teaching you to treat your elders with suitable respect.'

Elf's eyes snapped open again. To her relief, Richard's second head had disappeared. He was smiling with irritating arrogance now. He no longer looked forbidding, but she had no idea whether he was teasing her or not.

'Respect,' she scoffed. 'You mean grovlling deference, don't you? And anyway, you don't want to marry me.' Unwisely, she leaped to her feet. 'I mean you don't want to marry *me* specifically. You just need to fill an inconvenient vacancy in your bed——' She broke off as her head swirled dangerously, and she felt her body sag against the table.

'You are not,' said Richard, his voice sounding oddly distorted, 'in the least convenient, Elfriede. In my bed or anywhere else, as I believe I've mentioned before. And grovelling deference would do nicely.'

Elf raised her eyes, and saw that although he had spoken lightly his expression was about as soft as cold steel.

'In fact,' he continued when she reached down to pick up her wine glass, 'I have a feeling you're about to become exceedingly tiresome—and you have had more than enough of *that*.' He removed the glass from her hand with smooth dexterity and held it over his head.

Elf lunged for it, but Richard handed it calmly to a passing waiter. When she started to move round the table, he stood up, seized her wrists, and trapped both of them securely behind her back.

'Now listen here, Richard Laslo,' she began. 'I have had exactly one and a half glasses —— '

'No, you listen here, Elf Makepeace,' he interrupted, as he placed an arm firmly round her waist. 'I am not about to let you make an exhibition of yourself *or* me. And what you need at this moment is a brisk walk.'

'What I need is the rest of my wine. My stomach hurts.' Elf tried to pull away from him, but his grip on her waist only tightened.

Her head whirled alarmingly, but she decided she liked the feel of him against her side.

'Like hell you do,' growled Richard, steering her across the thick carpet, past the discreetly averted eyes of the staff and the discreetly observing eyes of the other diners. She staggered, and he glanced down at her sharply. 'Are you all right?'

'I don't know,' said Elf. 'I've been feeling funny ever since we arrived.'

Richard groaned and whisked her smartly outside. When the damp air hit her face, she tried to pull back, but he wouldn't let her. Instead he hurried her across the street so fast that her feet barely touched the ground— much to the entertainment of a convention of lady tourists in red trouser-suits who were on their way into the hotel.

He held her against him as the chattering red throng passed them by. Elf sighed and stumbled over the kerb.

'Straight back to your room, I think,' said Richard, pulling her upright the moment her body began to droop.

'Oh, no, I'm fine.' Her stomach lurched again, and she tripped over a crack in the pavement.

'I dare say—but, as I don't plan to spend the rest of the day holding you up, I'm afraid bed's your only option.'

'Mmm. Lovely idea,' agreed Elf, running languorous eyes over his long, streamlined body. Funny, her head was still twirling about, but her stomach seemed to have settled down nicely.

Richard looked grim, and muttered something she didn't catch as she swayed in the direction of the kerb again and narrowly avoided collision with a passing cyclist.

All at once Elf's temporary euphoria began to fade. A cool breeze stroked at her face, a fist seemed to twist in her insides, and she felt as if she were turning into a limp and sickly rag doll.

She thought she heard Richard sigh as he pushed her into the Rolls.

Suddenly she felt very tired, not giddy at all, and as if a bulldozer had rolled over her belly.

A little while later, just as she was drifting off to sleep, the Rolls pulled up in front of the Bonavista.

Richard leaned across her and opened the door. 'Out you get,' he ordered. Elf smiled and lolled back against the seat.

Muttering something which sounded like, 'God give me strength!' Richard flung open the driver's door, uncoiled his legs and walked round to Elf's side of the car.

Her eyes had closed again and, murmuring a few choice words, he put one arm around her shoulders and the other one under her knees. Then, pushing the door closed with his hip, he strode up the six steps of the Bonavista and deposited Elf unceremoniously on her feet.

'Where's your key?' he demanded, steadying her as she blinked owlishly up at him.

She started to search the pockets of her jacket. 'It's—I don't know.' She searched some more. 'Oh, how about that? It's right here.' She pulled the key out of the back pocket of her trousers and flashed him a triumphant beam.

'Remarkable,' murmured Richard. 'Give it to me.'

She did seem to be having trouble finding the lock, and, after mistaking a button on his shirt for the keyhole, she gave in and handed it over. Then, just as he was inserting it, pain twisted her intestines again, and without realising what she was doing she lurched away from him and stumbled back into the street.

The pain receded, and she looked up to see him turning around, his expression discouraging. The glitter in his eyes, she decided, was of the kind that promised her little joy. And suddenly she felt a devilish urge to provoke him.

Richard was so high and mighty, so certain of his own capability, and her incompetence... It would do him good to have his feathers ruffled.

She gave him a sidelong glance, and inched her way along the pavement. Behind her she heard him swear, and growl something about a walking disaster area, animated trouble on two legs. She supposed he meant her.

The next thing she knew, she was lying face down across his shoulder.

'Keep still,' he ordered, when automatically she started to struggle. 'Believe me, young lady, I have reached the point where if I don't do something about you soon—preferably something for which I may escape a charge of aggravated homicide—I am definitely going to lose my temper. *You* may lose a good deal more.'

'You're not being very gentlemanly,' complained Elf, smoothing her fingers down his spine. Vaguely she was conscious that his hand was on her bottom where it had no business. But it felt nice...

Then he was setting her upright on the steps, supporting her against his shoulder. 'And you,' he said grimly, 'are not much of a lady. In fact you're an exceptionally trying pain in the —'

'Definitely not a gentleman,' said Elf, sticking her tongue out.

A group of teenagers passing in the street stopped to stare, and Richard told her sternly that if she didn't behave herself he would be a lot more than ungentlemanly.

'Oh-h,' said Elf, pretending to shiver, and batting her eyelashes at him. 'Are you going to grab me by the hair and drag me off to your cave?'

'No,' said Richard, giving her a look of acute disfavour as the teenagers on the pavement broke into jeering laughter. 'I am going to grab you by the shoulders and any other part of your anatomy that's available—and drag you off to...' He paused, took a deep breath and finished. 'To get some sleep.'

'Oh,' sighed Elf. 'I thought you were going to suggest something nicer.'

'Not on your life,' he snapped.

The jeers from the street had now turned to encouraging catcalls, and, without further ado, Richard unlocked the door and shoved Elf ahead of him into the cluttered hall.

'Mmm,' murmured Elf. 'You feel nice against my back like that.' She leaned her head on his chest and tried to halt their progress, but Richard put two heavy hands on her shoulder-blades and told her to keep on walking.

'Walking,' echoed Spinach, the minah. 'Keep walking.'

Richard ignored him and marched Elf to the bottom of the stairs.

'Which room?' he asked, as Spinach shrieked after them to shut the door.

'Number nine.'

Before she could protest, he had scooped her over his shoulder again, and was carrying her up the steep Georgian stairs.

'All right, now we need another key,' he said, planting her outside the door of number nine. 'Where is it?'

Elf shrugged. She was feeling a little sick again. 'I don't know. You find it.'

Richard's lips tightened, but without arguing he rammed both hands into the pockets of her jacket. She felt the pressure of his fingers against her thighs. Maybe he wouldn't be able to find the key...

But he found it almost at once, and as soon as the door was unlocked he kicked it open, picked Elf up, and dumped her rather too heavily on to the big, canopied bed with the pink cover.

He bent over her to remove her jacket, and she smiled drowsily up at him. But, just as he touched her neck and began to unfasten the top button, a voice from the doorway made him pause.

'Here now,' it bellowed furiously. 'None of that, you two. This is a respectable establishment, I'll have you know.'

Richard stopped unbuttoning and dropped his hand to his side.

CHAPTER NINE

ELF watched as Richard pivoted slowly on his heel and turned a hard stare on the plump little man glowering at them from the doorway. He had beady black eyes that looked ready to pop straight out of his head.

'You needn't worry,' said Richard coldly. 'I can assure you the young lady is in no condition for "any of that".' His lip curled, and only Elf heard him add under his breath, 'Unfortunately.'

The proprietor of the Bonavista glared suspiciously, and Elf made a great effort to look dignified and aloof—a feat difficult to accomplish from a recumbent position on the bed, with her shoes on, and her head spinning in rainbow-coloured arcs.

'I'm perfectly all right, Mr Busby,' she assured him. 'And I'm also perfectly respectable.' She tried to wither him with a haughty stare, but that only made her head spin faster.

Mr Busby remained annoyingly un-withered. 'You'd better not be sick on my carpet,' he said belligerently. 'I don't allow drunk and disorderly in my rooms.'

'I'm not drunk,' said Elf. Then she abandoned dignity as a wave of nausea knocked her back on the pillows. 'I'm just ill.'

Richard frowned. 'Disorderly she may be at times,' he conceded, not looking at the indignant proprietor, 'but I'm beginning to think her condition owes more to a virus than to alcohol.'

'Virus?' muttered Elf. 'Is that why my head feels so funny?'

'Probably. And, in retrospect, I believe ordering wine was a mistake.'

Elf scarcely heard him. 'I think,' she said despairingly, 'that my halibut is about to swim back.'

Mr Busby made a choking noise and scurried out of the room, muttering something about cleaning bills for carpets over his shoulder. He slammed the door so forcefully that the windows rattled.

'I do believe our Mr Busby's sense of propriety has been vanquished by the probable return of your halibut,' murmured Richard, removing a handful of moth-eaten dried flowers from a bowl on her bedside table.

Elf started to giggle, but when Richard handed the bowl to her she was sick instead.

'Oh, Richard, I *am* so sorry,' she whispered a few minutes later, as he wiped her face with a towel he had found on the washbasin.

'So am I,' he agreed. 'But I'm not sure you're altogether to blame.'

Well, that's a change of tune, thought Elf, wondering if she had heard right. She decided not to press it. 'I expect it just happened because I'm tired,' she suggested hopefully. 'I feel better now.'

'Hmm.' Richard was sceptical. 'If you're in the habit of returning your meals every time you feel tired, Makepeace, remind me never to let you out of bed——'

'I'm not in the rabbit of returning my heals,' she interrupted drowsily. Why did her eyelids feel so heavy...?

Richard raised his eyes to the pink cherubs painted on the ceiling then bent down to remove her shoes.

As she drifted off into oblivion, Elf thought she heard the faint sound of a man trying to choke back a laugh.

When she awoke, the room was dark, and the glitter of starlight shone through a chink in the curtains. There was no sign of Richard.

Elf turned on the bedside lamp. Then she blinked. She could have sworn that when she fell asleep she had been wearing trousers and a bright yellow blouse—not the thin white nightgown she had on now. She moved her head tentatively. If felt quite normal. No dizziness, and the pain in her stomach had gone.

So what had happened? She'd been ill, Richard had brought her home, Mr Busby had been furious, and somehow in all the confusion someone had undressed her and put her to bed.

Richard. A slow flush crept up over her ears, and when she looked in the mirror she saw that her face was beginning to blend in nicely with the neon walls. Richard had taken her clothes off. All of them. And she hadn't been awake to enjoy it.

'Elf Makepeace,' she said out loud, horrified by her traitorous imaginings. '*What* are you thinking of?'

But she knew exactly what she'd been thinking of, so she got up hastily to pour herself a long, cold glass of water.

She finished it, and was just about to climb back into bed when the door was suddenly pushed open.

Elf looked up, gasped, tripped over a shaggy purple rug and ended up sprawled across the bed with her rear at an inelegant angle.

'Very tempting,' observed Richard, advancing into the room with a pot of tea on a tray. 'And I must say you've got it coming to you.'

Elf rolled over on to her back and sat up.

Richard put down the tray, filled a cup, and lowered himself down beside her.

'Here, drink this,' he said, putting an arm round her shoulders and holding the cup to her lips.

'I can't,' whispered Elf, who was totally at a loss to cope with the sensations cascading through her body as this autocratic and very sexy man settled himself casually on her bed as if it—and its occupant—were his property.

'Yes, you can. Come on. You've been ill, and you need something to warm you.'

Elf didn't tell him he was doing a nice job of warming her just by sitting there. 'I'm all

right,' she insisted. 'This afternoon I thought
I was going to die, but——'

'If you don't do as you're told and drink
this, you may very well die sooner than you
think,' he promised her. 'And I don't mean
in peace. However, as I have no urgent desire
to serve time for what other people might
quite unreasonably call murder—personally
I'd call it a public service—you will kindly
drink this *now*. Do I make myself clear?'

He did.

Elf eyed him warily, and took a sip. It tasted
warm and bracing, so she drank some more.

'That's better,' said Richard complacently.

It was too. Elf hadn't even realised she
needed bracing. 'Richard,' she said slowly,
wriggling her feet under the covers and pulling
the sheet up to her neck. 'Richard, did you
undress me?'

'Mmm.' He smoothed a hand over his jaw.

'Oh. I—er——'

'Don't worry, your virtue's still intact. I
prefer my women awake when I make love to
them.'

Elf wondered why he sounded so re-
proving. 'I didn't mean...' She hesitated.
What didn't she mean? That she wished she

had been awake? 'I wasn't worrying about my virtue,' she said quickly.

'Really? That's the most promising remark you've made all day.'

'But I am worrying about it now,' said Elf quickly. 'At least I would be if —— '

'If you were up to it?'

'*No.*' Elf sighed. In her present condition there was no way she would get the better of Richard in a war of words. The best thing to do was change the subject.

'Thank you for helping me,' she said, trying to sound as if having her clothes removed while she slept was of no great moment. 'Er— Richard?'

'Mmm?'

'Richard, what happened to me? One minute I was fine, and then I wasn't.'

He patted her thigh absently through the bedclothes. 'Flu,' he said. 'Sometimes it happens that way, so the doctor said.'

'Doctor?'

'Don't you remember? I had him in to check you over.'

'Oh.' Elf frowned. 'Yes, I guess I do remember a lot of fussing around. But I was half asleep.'

'Three-quarters asleep. Anyway, he said you'd probably live.' He stood up.

'Where are you going?' asked Elf.

'To return this tea-tray which our beetle-browed friend was exceedingly reluctant to part with—and then back to my flat to get some sleep. You'd better do the same. It's nearly midnight.'

'But I'm . . . Oh.' She had been about to say she was wide awake now, but Richard's face had a bruised, weary look about it, and it suddenly occurred to her that he was probably nearly dead on his feet. 'All right,' she finished, with a meekness that caused him to glance at her suspiciously.

A few minutes later, apparently satisfied that she wasn't about to head out for a night on the tiles, he touched a finger lightly to her nose, said 'Goodnight, daffodil,' and closed the door quietly behind him.

Elf expected she would lie awake for hours, but in fact her eyelids began to droop the moment Richard left the room, and, the next thing she knew, pink fingers of dawn were trailing over the brick roof across the road. In the soft, early morning light, the wallpaper looked almost natural and the toy tiger looked like a kitten.

She lay there for some time, watching the pink sky turn to orange, and when she eventually sat up the sun was well above the trees that lined the street.

To her surprise, she saw a small scrap of paper with writing on it tucked beneath the blue bowl beside her bed.

She lifted the bowl, which showed no sign of the unorthodox use to which it had been put the day before, and glanced curiously down at the writing. She read,

Good morning, Daffodil.

I hope your nightmares were sweet, and that your head feels no worse than you deserve. Be ready at eleven o'clock.

Richard.

P.S. After considerable reflection, I've come to the reluctant conclusion that it would be irresponsible of me to let you loose on my unsuspecting compatriots. You, my sweet, are sorely in need of a keeper. A September wedding will suit me quite well.

'Grr,' said Elf, to the stuffed tiger. 'Just because you undressed me, Richard Laslo, that *doesn't* mean you own me.'

A keeper indeed! Of course he had written that deliberately to provoke her, not because he particularly meant it, but even so...

An unwilling smile tugged at the corner of her mouth. Richard was good at provoking. He wasn't at all bad at undressing either, she conceded ruefully, as she took in that her trousers and blouse were folded neatly over a chair. Had he enjoyed that little operation? she wondered, smoothing a crease in the paper. No, probably he hadn't much. She could hardly have been responsive. On the other hand, he *had* asked—no, *told*—her to marry him. Again.

This was his third proposal. Unnecessarily, she counted on her fingers. And this one was in writing, so perhaps he meant it. But it still didn't make any sense. He had assured her he wanted a nice, unencumbering sort of wife. But yesterday she had been much more than a mere encumbrance...

Yes, and he had coped efficiently and quite kindly.

Elf blinked as a sunbeam struck the window and the wallpaper assaulted her as usual. A brief pain shot through her head. She closed her eyes and leaned back on the pillows— because along with the pain had come realisation.

She wanted to marry Richard more than she'd wanted anything in her life. So why did she keep on refusing him? It wasn't because she didn't know what she'd be getting into. In a way, she had known him most of her life— and the bossy, teasing little boy had turned into a bossy, infuriating, terminally sceptical adult who believed only in those things he could touch. But behind his scepticism and his autocractic manner she had glimpsed a strong, compassionate, essentially generous man—whom she happened to love.

So why was she holding back?

'That's easy, Elf, my girl,' she said to the tiger. 'One very important word, that's what's holding you back. It's called love.'

Yes, the love that Richard couldn't give her. Marriage to Felicity had destroyed his faith in the existence of the kind of love that made the world go round. The love she believed in and longed for.

Elf pulled at the neck of her nightgown. The question she had to answer now was, could she live with what Richard did have left to offer? He liked her well enough, she was sure of that. And he wanted her. Past experience might have blunted his ability to love, but not his belief in marriage as a desirable estate.

Perhaps love might grow from that beginning.

No. She mustn't delude herself. But perhaps *her* love might be enough for them both.

'All right. I'll do it,' she said out loud, her voice ringing out on a triumphant chord. 'I'll marry you, Richard Laslo.'

From the other side of the door Spinach let out a derisive screech.

'Just never you mind,' Elf shouted at him. 'I don't care what you think. I'm going to marry him anyway.'

When she heard her own voice bounce back at her, she started to laugh. Even if she had gone totally mad, she didn't care. When Richard arrived at eleven she would tell him, quite matter-of-factly, that she had thought over his proposal and made up her mind to accept him. What happened after that would lie in the lap of the gods.

Elf stretched her arms over her head, feeling as if a dense cloud had lifted from her mind. Smiling to herself, she swung her legs on to the floor. Richard was coming at eleven—and soon she, Elf Makepeace, would be his wife.

She dressed quickly in fitted white trousers and a low-cut canary-yellow shirt, and by eleven o'clock she was poised by the door waiting for Richard's summons.

At noon she was still in her room, but sitting tensely on the edge of the bed.

By half-past twelve she had decided she would give him till one, conveniently forgetting that in the days of Tony and Harry it had been one of her firmest principles never to wait longer than half an hour for her escort to pick her up.

She waited until half-past one before throwing her bag over her shoulder and flinging open the door with such force that the rush of air swishing through the hall caused Spinach to say loudly, 'Wake up.'

'And boiling oil to you,' Elf retorted as she stomped down the stairs and out into the pouring rain. 'Man-eating ants. Mumps. It doesn't matter, because all of them are too good for you, Richard Laslo.'

Spinach screeched again as she closed the door.

It was obvious now that in the sober light of morning Richard had thought better of his proposal and decided he could manage very well without a wife who was sick into boarding-house flower bowls—and needed a keeper.

Well, she could do without him too.

Scowling at a startled ticket-taker, she marched down the steps to the Underground while she contemplated the damage that could sometimes be wrought by mumps on the capabilities of virile young men. She didn't know if Richard had ever had mumps, but if he hadn't they would do just fine. Besides, there weren't many man-eating ants in London, and boiling oil wasn't likely to be sold in the average shop.

Elf's anger and disappointment carried her through most of the day in a relentless continuation of yesterday's interrupted sightseeing. She even tried to find the house in Fulham where her mother had lived as a child. But when an elderly man told her it had been

pulled down to make way for new apartments
she wasn't surprised.

'I might have known,' she said to him
sourly. 'Nothing else has gone right since I
came to London.'

The man muttered something about people
who came all this way to complain being
welcome to go back where they came from.
Elf saw his point.

At last, worn out by her own militant
tourism, she was forced to stop for a cup of
tea in a small café near St Paul's Cathedral.
And there, as she gazed with gloomy uninterest at a family of six devouring currant
buns, it suddenly came to her that there was
one possibility she hadn't even stopped to
consider.

What if she had been too quick to judge
Richard? What if his Rolls had developed an
unlikely mechanical problem and crashed? Or
what if he had slipped on the rain-slicked
streets and broken something?

She stirred a spoonful of salt abstractedly
into her tea. Why hadn't she thought of that
before? She wasn't usually so quick to jump
to conclusions. Richard was irritating to a
degree when he wanted to be, but he had a

habit of keeping his word. If he'd changed his mind about meeting her, he would surely have felt obliged to let her know.

She took a quick mouthful of tea, choked, and put her hand to her mouth.

'Something wrong, dear?' An anxious little waitress bustled up. 'Are you all right?'

'Yes, yes, I'm fine thanks,' gasped Elf. 'I— er—I mistook the salt for the sugar.'

'Of course, dear,' said the waitress, as if her customers routinely salted their tea. 'I'll fetch you a fresh cup.'

Elf accepted the fresh tea gratefully, gulped it down, and hurried back into the street. It was still raining. She glanced at her watch. Four o'clock. Laslo's would still be open, and there was an Underground stop at Bond Street. She'd looked it up. If anything had happened to Richard, surely his staff would be the first to know.

Half an hour later she was standing across the street from Laslo's waiting for a gap in the traffic. When it came, she put out a tentative foot.

But a flash of bright hair on the other side of the street caught her eye, and she paused, gaping. Then she clutched frantically at a lamp-post, stumbled over her feet and almost fell in front of a passing car.

She squeezed her eyes shut, opened them again, swallowed. No, she wasn't dreaming. Not twenty feet in front of her on a side-street, a man and a woman were entering a doorway. Above it hung a sign which read, 'One For the Road Bar and Grill.'

The woman had a cloud of auburn hair and a swaying, provocative gait. The man had waving fair hair and the most seductive shoulders Elf had ever set eyes on. And she ought to know, because last night they had supported her head.

Now it was Miranda's hair that swung intimately against Richard's arm while his fingers curved lightly round her elbow. He was looking down at her with an expression that from this distance Elf couldn't make out.

But she had no doubt whatever that it reflected anticipation of pleasures yet to be taken. She had been totally mistaken about Richard. He wasn't immune to big blue eyes and cleavage after all.

CHAPTER TEN

ELF took a step forward, feeling her teeth bite into her lower lip. But the absorbed couple on the other side of the street had disappeared into One for the Road.

Should have been 'One for the Toad', Elf thought venomously. Almost immediately shock had given way to intense hurt, and then to rage. How *could* Richard do this to her? She had wasted a futile morning waiting for him to come for her, then spent the last hour tortured by visions of him lying bandaged in a hospital bed—while all the time the snake had been cavorting round London with Miranda. And she had believed him when he'd said the redhead wasn't his style. Believed him implicitly.

She tightened her fingers on the lamp-post and took a long, controlling breath. If Richard thought he was going to get away with this, he didn't know Elfriede Makepeace. Not by a long shot, he didn't.

As she dodged traffic and ran across the road, Elf thought briefly of the note he had written her only last night—and the knife in her heart twisted, made her double over in pain.

Brakes squealed and a woman swore. Straightening herself with an effort, Elf stepped round an advancing taxi and gained the kerb.

A few seconds later, with her fingers digging holes in her palms, she pushed open the door through which she had seen her quarry vanish, and glanced quickly around the crowded, noisy room.

At first she couldn't see much as her eyes adjusted to the dimness. Then someone moved at a table in a shadowy corner, and she saw the light catch Richard's mane of hair.

He and Miranda were seated across from each other nursing white wine and whisky respectively. Elf stared, jolted out of her grief and rage just long enough to note that Richard wasn't gazing hotly into the beauty's eyes as she'd expected, but glaring with tight-lipped concentration at his glass. Miranda, true to form, was smiling sweetly and leaning across the table at an angle calculated to deliver the maximum dose of her assets.

'Richard, *darling*...' Elf heard her coo as she approached their corner.

'Yes, isn't he?' Elf pulled up a chair and thumped herself down between them. 'Also a snake and a toad and a ——'

'Lizard?' suggested Richard helpfully, withdrawing his gaze from the glass with unruffled detachment.

Elf glowered.

'Just continuing the reptilian metaphor,' he explained amiably.

'Shut up,' she snapped, abandoning any vague notion of attempting to control her temper. How dared he? Instead of apologising, or showing any sign of contrition, Richard actually seemed to be enjoying this appalling scene. 'Besides,' she added, her chin tilting aggressively, 'the comparison is unfair to reptiles.' The look she flashed him then would have reduced Tony—and even Harry—to shamefaced acknowledgement of guilt.

It only inspired Richard to further heights of provocation. 'And amphibians,' he corrected languidly. 'Toads are amphibians, I believe.'

Elf's face turned an unattractive shade of brick, and she knew that if she didn't do something drastic she would scream.

Miranda chose that moment to decide she'd been ignored long enough. 'Really, Elf,' she began, 'I do think —— '

'No, you don't,' interrupted Elf, by this time goaded beyond good sense. 'Thinking isn't one of your accomplishments—unless you're under the impression that your brain is located in your —— '

'Elf!' Richard's voice was no longer detached, and his words cracked across the table like gunshot. 'Stop behaving like an idiot. I'm sorry I missed you this morning, but, as you ought to have known, there was a reason —— '

'I know now though, don't I?' Elf interrupted. 'Her name's Miranda Bannington.'

Richard's mouth hardened, and Miranda's blue eyes shot daggers of ice across the table.

But Richard wasn't looking at Miranda. He was gripping the arms of his chair as if he needed to hold on to something to prevent himself from taking Elf by the shoulders and shaking her. When she looked into his eyes, the possibility that he might be about to do just that didn't seem entirely far-fetched. She flinched away from him, then remembered that he was a supposedly civilised man having

a drink in a civilised bar. She took a firm grip
on herself.

'Listen to me, Richard,' she began.

'No. You listen to me. And kindly stop
playing the jilted bride. The part doesn't suit
you. Let me tell you, Miss——'

'No, let me tell *you*,' Elf shouted, jumping
to her feet and planting her palms flat on the
table. She leaned towards him so that their
eyes were only inches apart. 'I'm telling you
that there's no way I'm playing the bride,
jilted or otherwise, because if I ever have *any*
inclination to get married—which I very
much doubt—it will not, and I mean *not*, in
any circumstances, be to you.'

'No, said Richard. 'I see it won't.' His face
was impassive. He had himself under control
now, but she saw that his skin had turned unusually wax-like.

'Good. Maybe this will make you see even
better.'

Elf seized Miranda's glass of wine just as
the redhead was reaching for it, and raised it
as far as her shoulder.

What would have happened next she wasn't
sure. She had barely time to form the intent
to throw it, before Richard's arm shot out,
caught her wrist, and with one quick twist re-

moved the liquid weapon from her grasp and gave it back to Miranda. Not a single drop spilled on the table.

Elf, slightly appalled at what she had been about to do, staggered backwards and grabbed blindly for a chair.

When Richard stood up and came towards her, instead of waiting to see what he meant to do she pushed back the chair and fled. Vaguely, as she reached the door, she heard the sound of his voice calling after her. The words he was using were original, and not likely to be found in a school dictionary.

Breathing hard, Elf ran outside and collapsed limply against the grey brick wall while she fought to dispel the blinding mist which had formed in front of her eyes.

She couldn't see, and the drizzle dampening her hair only added to her misery and disillusion.

'Elf,' rasped a voice in her ear. She jumped, as a heavy hand descended on to her shoulder.

She tried to pull away, but long fingers were digging into the fabric of her jacket, and she found herself pinned in Richard's grasp as brilliant green eyes blazed down at her, and lips that had once touched hers softly parted in an ominous white grimace.

Elf's heart began to thunder in her ears, as again she attempted to shake him off. But he only moved closer, his chest and legs pressing her to the wall.

And, incredibly, she found she didn't want to struggle any more.

As a solitary drop of rain trickled icily down her neck the anger slowly drained out of her, to be replaced by an enervating reluctance to move—or even to think. She only knew that she wanted to retreat into the shelter of her room, curl up in a safe little ball on her bed and pull the pillow over her head to block out all sensation, all hopes and dreams—and to banish the consciousness of Richard's hard body close to hers, and the touch of his fingers on her skin.

But that same body barred her escape, and as his thighs shifted against hers she knew that she could never block out all sensation. Not where this man was concerned.

'And what the hell was the meaning of that little exhibition?' he asked bitingly, his face so close to hers that his breath was fanning her cheek. 'I told you there was a reason I couldn't reach you this morning... *No*,' he ground out as Elf opened her mouth to protest. 'The reason is *not* Miranda. I tried to get hold of you —— '

'If you say so,' said Elf dully. 'I waited all morning.'

'I know, and I've told you I'm sorry. I'm not going to tell you again. The point is —— '

'It doesn't matter what the point is,' Elf said tiredly.

It didn't either, because even if Richard had a rock-solid reason for standing her up—and now that the fire had gone out of her she was beginning to believe that he had—the sight of him with Miranda had forced her to accept the one thing she hadn't wanted to acknowledge.

She couldn't marry Richard. She loved him too much. And, no matter how she tried to convince herself that her love would be enough for them both, when it came right down to it she knew now that it just wasn't true. He had been married to Felicity for nine years. He'd said they were friends—and she had seen for herself that he cared about her. Now he expected to marry again, to give his new wife a secure home, perhaps her own business to run, and maybe a child or two. But beyond that, for all his wealth, Richard couldn't give her the one thing that mattered. Married to him, she would still be alone. And she wouldn't be able to bear it. Seeing him today with Miranda had shown her that.

'It doesn't matter,' she repeated, running the back of her hand across her eyes. 'If you say you didn't mean to let me down, I believe you. At least I think I do. I can even believe you're not remotely interested in Miranda, that there's a reasonable explanation for why you're with her. I'm sorry I reacted without thinking. But—Richard, I—I don't want to marry you. It's better if we say goodbye now, before things go any further. I'm—fond of you, truly I am, and I'm honoured that you asked me to be your wife, even if —— '

'Even if what?' His breath was warm on her cheek, but his voice was cold and contained.

'Even if it's not a good idea,' she finished lamely, staring at his blue striped tie and seeing the rain darken the grey of his jacket.

'I'm beginning to think you're right.' The words were harsh, bitten off, and she glanced up doubtfully because although he was agreeing with her he was making no attempt to move away. And he didn't sound agreeable, he sounded hard and angry.

Something which was neither grief nor hurt began to stir in her then. Something that made her want to throw her arms round his neck to pull the sinuous length of him closer. But when she looked into his eyes she saw no answering hunger. Only a bleak, icy control that tore at her heart.

'Goodbye, Richard,' she whispered, pressing her hands against his shirt. It was damp. His body was protecting her from the worst of the rain, but he was soaked. She moved her fingers and felt his muscles contract through the wetness. 'Don't catch cold.' Her admonition came out on a choking sob and she wasn't sure he had heard her.

She gave his chest a desperate shove, half expecting, half hoping he would remain as solid and immovable as she had reason to know he could be.

But he made no effort to detain her and stepped smoothly, wordlessly backwards. No answering goodbye, no farewell kiss. Nothing.

Just before she turned away Elf caught a brief glimpse of his face. It was very still, not a muscle moving. Like a statue carved out of ice. And yet—and yet behind the stillness hadn't there been something—some emotion rigidly suppressed? Something that looked almost like—pain? As well as anger.

No, she must have been mistaken. It was just the rain glistening on his skin, creating an illusion. She clasped her black shoulder-bag tightly and began to run down the street.

Her pounding footsteps sounded very loud in the damp evening air, and she almost collided with a woman backing out of a doorway. She slowed, and for a second thought she heard the thud of even louder footsteps pursuing her—but it must have been her imagination because when she rounded the corner into Bond Street she heard only her own feet slapping unevenly against the wet pavement.

There was no one pursuing her.

Richard, one shoulder resting against the wall, watched as Elf's retreating figure blended into the rain. For a long time he stared, unmoving, at the place where she had vanished from his sight.

After several minutes he straightened, turned back to the bar, and slammed his fist hard against the doorpost. He remembered, grimly, that Elf had always been the type who fought back, whether her wrongs were real or imagined. He thought of her eyes, black and furious, when she'd lifted that glass to aim it at his head...

Glaring into the crowded room, he strode towards a pouting Miranda, who by now, he supposed, was also itching for a stand-up fight.

If she was, she was likely to get it.

Elf stumbled up the steps of the Bonavista and fiddled ineffectually with her key. Finally, after a lot of groping, complicated by the tears that she could no longer hold back, she managed to fit it into the lock.

'Humbug,' said Spinach, as she passed his cage and pushed open the door to her room.

'Humbug indeed,' agreed Elf, letting it close slowly behind her and collapsing against a neon-pink wall.

She crossed her arms and stared morosely at the tiger, whose yellow eyes stared back balefully.

At first she was too stunned to move, too tortured by the decision she had made. It would be so easy now to change her mind, to tell Richard she hadn't meant it...

'Elf Makepeace, stop it at once.' She wiped a hand wearily over her eyes and pushed herself away from the wall. 'He didn't even try to make you stay.' When the tiger continued to glare, she realised she was talking to herself. But it made no difference. If she went back on her decision now, then all the hope, the pain, the doubt and unhappiness would start again. It was time to get away from this cluttered room with its painful memories, and learn to get on with her life. Because if she stayed here, in spite of herself she would spend her days wondering if Richard would call—hoping he wouldn't and yet secretly praying that he would.

And the uncertainty would defeat her in the end.

She couldn't allow that to happen.

With slow, weighted movements Elf pulled her suitcases out from under the bed.

An hour later she explained to a surprisingly sympathetic Mr Busby that she was very sorry, but something had come up and she had to leave.

'Good riddance,' shouted Spinach at her departing back.

Elf stood forlornly in the street beside her cases and stared blankly at a cigarette butt smouldering in the gutter. How was it that she, who had always been so capable of handling her own problems, felt totally lost and alone? She had changed in the past week, no doubt about it. For one thing, the woman she had been a week ago would never have made that scene in One for the Road.

And if that's what love does to people, she thought bitterly, it's a good thing Richard's out of my life.

In spite of the heaviness around her heart, she knew she had to keep believing that.

Three weeks, thought Elf, staring round the dingy brown room. Has it really been only three weeks since I saw Richard? It seems a lifetime.

A lifetime during which she had stayed in several dingy rooms just like this one, and embarked on a bus tour to Scotland. Now she was back in London, and conscious every moment that Richard was just a train ride away. She wondered if he thought of her at all...

A mouse skittered across the floor. Elf watched it disappear behind a rickety dresser, and knew she had to get away from these dreary quarters. Besides, the sun was out for a change. Perhaps if she went for a long walk she would sleep tonight, and win a few hours of forgetting.

It was a warm and peaceful summer evening, and as she strolled along the busy streets on her way to Kensington Gardens Elf felt a faint lightening of her spirits. But when she reached the park, her gaze fell on a pair of lovers, blissfully entwined on the grass. Another couple, totally absorbed in each other, stood beside the Serpentine kissing.

Elf brushed a tear from her eye and felt even more desolate than before.

Suddenly she could bear it no longer.

As if they had minds of their own, her feet began to take a new direction. She began to walk faster, took a wrong turn, and, after backtracking twice, found her way to the Mayfair mews she was unwilling to admit was her destination. When she reached number seven, she paused. *Was* it seven she had read on the label on Richard's briefcase? Yes, it had to be. Because if it wasn't....

Taking a deep breath, Elf raised her hand to the brass knocker.

It seemed a very long time before anyone came, but at last the door was pulled open by a neat middle-aged woman with a wide mouth. She gave Elf a friendly smile and didn't seem at all surprised to see a pink-faced, slightly breathless young lady blinking up at her from the shadows.

Elf gulped. 'Er—is—is this Mr Laslo's residence?' she asked in a suffocated voice.

'Yes, it is,' the woman replied pleasantly. 'But I'm afraid he's out.'

'Oh.' Elf felt as if she'd been told the world had ended.

Her despair must have shown on her face, because the wide mouth parted to add at once, 'I don't think he'll be long, though. He's in the middle of an important appraisal. Won't you come in? He said he was just going for a quick work-out at the gym.'

Elf swallowed and murmured doubtful thanks as she stepped dazedly over the threshold. Maybe she was making a mistake, but she had come this far, and it would be senseless to turn tail and run.

'I'm Jean,' explained the older woman. 'Mr Laslo's secretary.' She gave a small sigh. 'He asked me to come in tonight to help him work on the appraisal. Come and sit down.'

She led Elf into a bare, white-walled room with a grey carpet running beneath a black leather sofa. One straight-backed chair was pushed against a solid teak desk and two futuristic prints hung on the wall, both of them

in shades of black and grey. The impression
was bleak, cold and unwelcoming.

'It's very—er—practical, isn't it?' said Elf.
'Is the rest of the house like this?'

'More or less, but with a bit more colour.
It was this way in his uncle's day, and Mr
Laslo just never bothered to change it.' Jean
tossed her head. 'In my opinion, what this
place needs is a woman's touch. But that wife
of his never came near it. Always at their
country house, she was, fussing about with
her horses. Not that he ever said much.'

'No,' said Elf. 'He wouldn't.' She perched
herself gingerly on the edge of the sofa.

Jean sat down on the chair in front of the
desk and glanced shrewdly at Elf's drawn little
face. 'Know him well, do you?'

'No, no, not really...'

'Hm. Well I can tell you he's turned into a
regular workaholic lately. Never stops.' She
rolled her eyes up. 'Of course he was always
an exacting employer, but these days he has
about as much patience as a hungry shark. If
he keeps it up, I'll be looking for another job,
let me tell you. And soon.'

'Oh, dear,' said Elf, wondering if Richard's
secretary was always this frank with his vis-

itors. Illogically, she felt a faint stirring of hope.

The phone rang and Jean picked it up. 'Yes?' she said. 'Miss Kelsey. You'll be free on Saturday. At seven. Yes, I'll tell him.' She shuffled some papers on the desk. 'Oh, just a moment. I see he's dining with young Lady Keating on Saturday —— ' She broke off as a stream of words—angry from the sound of them—burst out of the receiver like bullets. When the noise stopped, Jean said with icy politeness, 'Yes, Miss Kelsey. I'll tell him.' She put down the phone and wiped a hand over her brow.

'Mr Laslo's—er—social life, sounds—complicated,' murmured Elf, trying to prevent her voice from cracking.

'Huh. I don't know about social life, but he's no hermit, if that's what you mean. Far from it. As for that Miss Kelsey...' Jean made her mouth as small as possible and gave Elf the impression that she'd suddenly turned into a clam.

'I see.' Elf stared at her feet. She felt as if a lump of ice had settled on her heart. And Jean might draw the line at discussing Richard's love-life, but she didn't have to discuss it. The picture was altogether clear.

Elf looked at the square white clock on the desk. It was getting late, Richard would be back soon, and she couldn't think what had possessed her to come to his flat in the first place. Nothing had changed. Seeing him, saying goodbye again, could only add to her misery. Better to leave things as they were.

'I must be going,' she said, abandoning her perch on the sofa. 'Thanks for asking me in, Jean, but I'm afraid I can't stay any longer.'

'Oh, but I'm sure Mr Laslo would like to see you. I hope it wasn't anything I said —— ' Jean's hand flew to her mouth.

'No, of course not. I'm just an acquaintance really. I met Richard once, that's all, and as I happened to be in the area . . .'

'Oh, I see.' Jean looked crestfallen. 'That's too bad. I thought—never mind, I expect I talk too much. I'll tell him you called, Miss . . . ?'

'Don't worry.' Elf shook her head. 'He won't be interested. Thank you again, Jean.' Without pausing for an answer she hurried past the bewildered secretary and ran down the steps to the street.

By the time she got back to her squalid room she was able to see it without peering through a curtain of tears.

She told herself she'd known all along that Richard was an attractive man who was only capable of skin-deep commitment. So he wasn't a hermit! What else had she expected? Surely not that love for her was the cause of his current black mood?

Staring down at the threadbare brown carpet that didn't quite cover the floor, she knew she'd been crazy to go to his flat. Totally out of her mind. But she'd recovered from that fit of madness now.

It was over.

The next day she booked her flight home.

Three days of frantic activity followed, during which Elf bought enough souvenirs for Sandra to fill a bathtub, and arranged to spend her final night in London at a smart modern hotel near Piccadilly. She'd had enough of living within her means.

But when she arrived at the registration desk she was told her room wasn't ready, so she sat down to wait on a straight-backed chair by the wall, and gazed incuriously round the spacious, carpeted lobby. After a while she put her feet up on her luggage and closed her eyes. When she opened them again a small man with a nondescript sort of face was staring at her from an alcove by the door. His look made her uncomfortable, so she stood up to make her way back to the reception desk.

'Evening, miss.' Elf jumped and turned to find that while she had been dozing in her chair a party of hefty young men had erupted into the lobby. She gaped, as the friendly one who had spoken to her was joined by a dozen or so others. The next moment she found herself surrounded by a sea of jostling red football sweaters as an exuberant team converged upon the desk.

'Good evening,' she replied hastily, accepting the key that a harried receptionist handed over.

The burly young man smiled and attempted to ease her way through the confusion of athletes. But at the edge of the circle she paused to adjust her shoulder-bag—and her hand froze on the strap.

Striding through the heavy glass doors held for him by a uniformed doorman was a tall, fair-haired man in a white sweater.

Elf closed her eyes. It couldn't be...

She forced herself to take another look.

It was.

With an audible gasp she stepped backwards. The football players were still milling around her, but she scarcely noticed them. Her attention was fixed on the arresting figure now standing just inside the door.

Hard green eyes met hers. No longer conscious of what she was doing, Elf took another step backwards, not noting or caring that she had put her foot through the looping handle of a red sports bag which its owner had tossed on the floor. When her ankle caught, she automatically kicked out to shake herself free, but the bag swivelled round and hit her on the leg, making her stumble.

Elf flung out her arms, fighting to regain her balance. But it was too late. Before she realised what was happening, the floor of the lobby was on its way up to meet her, and the football sweaters, the gathering crowd and the man who had been by the door dissolved into a riot of crimson stars.

CHAPTER ELEVEN

THE stars changed from crimson to scarlet and the football sweaters began to come back into focus. 'I think I'm alive,' Elf murmured.

One of the sweaters laughed, and she realised she was lying in an undignified heap on a blue carpet surrounded by a bevy of anxious beefcake.

And Richard was somewhere near. No. No, he couldn't be. She must have dreamed that.

'Nice work, Elf, my love,' drawled a familiarly biting voice. 'If you *had* to fall flat on your face in public, I'll admit you couldn't have collected a more impressive audience. Congratulations.'

That didn't sound like a dream. It sounded like Richard.

Elf moved her head. It hurt. The impressive audience shuffled and muttered suspiciously, but parted to let the newcomer through. He made his way swiftly to Elf's side and bent over her. She remembered, foggily, that it was the sight of Richard coming

265

through the hotel doorway that had caused her to trip in the first place. Out of habit she reached for something to throw. But when her fingers closed around nothing more substantial than a nest of carpet fluff all she could do was announce sharply that she wasn't flat on her face, thank you, as any idiot ought to be able to see.

What she wanted to say was, I love you. Please don't leave me again. But she couldn't make her lips form the words.

'I know,' conceded Richard. 'You're flat on your backside.' He dropped to one knee beside her. 'And a very neat one it is. But in the interests of tact...'

'Tact?' moaned Elf, wishing she didn't feel so queer and light-headed. 'You don't know the meaning of the word.'

'Don't I?' Richard seemed more interested in probing a tender spot just beside her right eye than in defending his diplomatic skills.

'Ouch,' said Elf, lifting her hand and feeling the egg-shaped protrusion on her temple.

'I should think so,' he agreed drily. 'I also think you ought to be in bed, at least until we're sure there's no concussion.' He put an

arm beneath her shoulders and another under
her knees and swung her up into his arms.

'You all right, miss?' asked a footballer,
fixing Richard with a pugnacious blue eye.

'Yes,' said Elf. 'I'm fine.'

It was true. In spite of a pounding headache
and a painful bump on her forehead, she was
more than all right. She was ecstatic, happy,
bemused and delighted and not at all sure she
was awake.

That day outside One for the Road she had
come, with anguish in her heart, to the bitter
conclusion that she would never marry, that
she would spend what was left of her life
alone. Because the only man she wanted
didn't love her. But now he was here, holding
her, and in his eyes there was a look of such
tender concern that in spite of herself—no,
because of herself—she had to hope.

Even if hope turned out to be a dream.

She buried her face in the white sweater. It
felt real. Warm and soft and subtly redolent
of man. She gave herself up to its warmth,
content for now to take each moment as it
came.

A well dressed couple stepping out of the
lift gaped in astonishment as the tall man

carried his burden aboard and pressed the button.

'I expect they think you're kidnapping me,' she murmured.

'I am,' he said shortly. 'And if you give me one more bit of trouble, my girl, I may lock you up and throw away the key.'

'But——'

'I mean it. You've led me quite a dance, Elfriede Makepeace. But if you have any doubts at all that the waltz is over, believe me, it won't take me long to change your mind.'

Elf did believe him. When he bent his head and brushed his lips over hers, she was sure that if she had been standing her legs would have collapsed underneath her. Her senses absorbed his heady, masculine scent and she clung to him as if he were a lifeline thrown to rescue her from drowning. As perhaps, in one sense, he was.

The lift doors opened and another gaping couple sidled past them with glances of startled disapproval.

'My reputation will be ruined,' muttered Elf.

'Too bad.' Richard removed the key she was still clutching and unlocked the door to a large room with a king-sized bed, two capacious dusky-pink armchairs and a carpet of hotel beige.

'This is becoming a habit,' he remarked, as he strode across the floor, laid her on the big bed, and began to pull off her shoes.

'What's becoming a habit?' She felt dazed, unable to get things into focus.

'Putting you to bed. Not that it's done me much good. So far.'

'What sort of good?' asked Elf sleepily.

He shrugged, and, seeing the way his eyes flicked over her limp body sprawled across the bed, she found that she was wide awake after all—and very much aware of exactly what sort of good he had in mind.

He sat down beside her as though he had every right, but, when he suddenly turned his head away as though he couldn't bear to look at her, she studied his aquiline profile with a puzzled frown. He looked older than when she had last seen him, and his face was thinner, as though he'd been ill...

'Richard,' she asked, 'why in the world are you here?'

Something about the words seemed familiar. She shook her head, which still felt fragile, and tried to remember where she'd spoken them before. Then it came to her. Of course. The shop with the tartan panties. History was repeating itself, and once again, in spite of her reservations, she was helplessly happy to see Richard Laslo. Which was ridiculous, she told herself, because the problems which had caused her to flee from him in the first place had not in any way been resolved.

'What *are* you doing here?' she repeated.

'At the moment I'm smoothing your fevered brow.' He suited action to words and placed a cool hand over her forehead. His touch was light, unlike the expression on his face, which was unnervingly sober.

'I don't feel fevered any more,' objected Elf. 'Or concussed.' She pushed his hand away and sat up. 'What I mean is, what brought you to *this* hotel? Of all places?' She was afraid of what his answer might be, but she had to know.

'You did,' he said grimly. When Elf's only response was a confused frown, he touched his thumb to the furrows between her eyebrows and went on, 'I let you get away from me that day because I was angry enough to scalp you, and I knew that if I caught up with you at once I was likely to do something we'd both regret. But when I went to the Bonavista the next day to settle the score —— '

'I'd gone,' said Elf in a small voice.

'Precisely. Your Mr Busby told me he thought you'd flown home. Which did nothing to improve my disposition, let me tell you. I had a lot of work to catch up on, and I knew it would be several weeks before I'd be free to fetch you back.'

'Fetch me back?'

'That's what I said. Dear heaven, Elf, it took me long enough to realise...' He stopped. 'Did you honestly think I'd give you up that easily?'

'I—yes, I suppose I did.'

'Well, you thought wrong. But I couldn't leave right away. Then Jean told me a young lady had called, and I knew from her description it was you.' He laid his hand on her thigh. 'Once I learned you were still in London, it didn't take my people long to track you down. Fortunately I was able to provide them with your picture—the fishy one—and they phoned me the moment they found you.' Richard spoke as if any other course of action would have been unthinkable, not as if it gave him satisfaction.

Elf wrinkled her nose. 'You mean you had me followed? Oh. Of course.' Suddenly everything fell neatly into place. 'The creepy little man with the flat eyes.'

'Mm. Creepy or not, he saved me a great deal of trouble. And when I came through those doors just now and saw a curly brown head going down for the count surrounded by the best display of muscular manpower I've seen in a long time . . .' He shook his head disgustedly. 'Naturally it had to be you.'

Elf aimed a fist at his chest. But he caught it and pushed it down by her side. 'No, you don't, daffodil,' he said, in a voice that told her he meant it. 'I've had all the nonsense I'm about to take from you.'

'Hey, you can't——' began Elf. But the sentence was never completed because Richard lowered his long body over hers and began to kiss her with an excruciating thoroughness that turned even the thought of resistance into water. By the time he'd finished she had forgotten what it was he couldn't do. She hadn't, however, forgotten why this shouldn't be happening.

'Miranda,' she managed to mutter, as he slid his hand purposefully down her hips and over her thighs. It wasn't what she'd meant to say, but somehow she couldn't bring herself to tell him about the revelation that had come to her as she leaned against a grey-brick London wall in the pouring rain. She couldn't *beg* him to love her. Miranda wasn't the problem, but she certainly brought it into focus.

Richard rolled off the bed as if she'd bitten him, and rose agilely on to his feet. 'What *about* Miranda?' he snapped, turning his back on her. 'You do know how to spoil a promising moment, don't you, Elf?'

Elf saw that the hands which only seconds before had been caressing her were balled into white-knuckled fists. She eyed them warily. 'It's all very well to talk about promising moments,' she said tightly. 'But I don't see anything promising about—about...' She didn't know how to explain to him that her dilemma really had very little to do with Miranda.

Richard whipped round to face her, his eyes a curious shade of olive. 'Elf,' he said in a dangerously controlled voice, 'what is this fixation about Miranda? Can't you credit me with sufficient judgement to know the difference between gold-digging, gift-wrapped trouble like Miranda Bannington—and an infuriating, elusive, obtuse but essentially generous-hearted woman called Elfriede Makepeace?'

Elf swallowed. 'I did—I do give you credit. I believed you when you said you had a reason for standing me up. But by then it didn't matter, because you didn't—don't, I didn't think you...' She couldn't finish.

'You didn't think I loved you,' he spoke in a low, gravelly voice that, unaccountably, tore at her heart.

'No,' she said sadly. 'I knew you didn't.'

He gave her a quick, hard smile and raked his hand through his hair. 'You were right, of course. I didn't. But, from the moment I heard a sweet voice behind me saying ''rats'' that day in New York, I had a feeling my life would never be the same. I felt winded. As if someone had just kicked me in the ribs—and I didn't much like it.'

Nothing had changed between them, but, watching his strong face etched sharply in the light from the window, Elf found herself beginning to hope. Something frozen inside her began to thaw.

'I often wanted to kick you,' she observed reflectively.

'The feeling was mutual.' He slid his hands into his pockets and rocked himself back on his heels.

Elf eyed him pensively. He didn't look threatening exactly, but his jaw was thrust out aggressively, and he looked very male, very exciting and very desirable.

'Richard,' she said slowly, 'I know you want me in a physical way, but...'

He took a step towards the bed and stood over her. 'But *what*, Elf? Why are there always "buts" with you? Damn it...' He paused, took a deep breath. 'OK. It's Miranda, isn't it? You can't get it into that thick curly head of yours that she means nothing to me.'

'No,' said Elf, shaking her head back and forth on the pillow. 'It's not that. Even though you did stand me up for her —— '

Richard swore. 'I did *not* stand you up for her,' he rasped, so forcefully that the glass on the washbasin rattled. 'It may have escaped your memory, but I'd already asked *you* to marry me. Bigamy isn't one of my vices.'

Elf put a hand to her head. It had started throbbing again. 'I didn't think it was,' she told him. 'But —— '

Richard groaned. 'Not another "but",' he muttered, striding over to the door and leaning against it as if he needed support. 'All right, my sweet affliction, apparently it's time

I made things clear. Firstly, I did not stand you up. It so happens that one of your fellow-countrymen made the mistake of driving on the right-hand side of the road as he does at home. The result was an unfortunate dust-up at Hyde Park Corner between my Rolls and his rented Range Rover. I didn't find it especially amusing, but happily there was no great damage done—except that by the time we had the whole mess sorted out the woman I intended to marry had disappeared. So I went back to my flat feeling a bit as though I'd survived a shipwreck, only to have my life-raft hijacked by a whale. In other words, I faced the dreary prospect of spending the day without you.'

'Oh,' said Elf.

He gave her a smile that did nothing to put her mind at rest, and added drily, 'Obviously I didn't have the sense to know I was well off. So I decided I'd better go in to work, and Jean, proving herself a very unsatisfactory dragon, allowed Miss Bannington to swivel her hips into my office.'

'You weren't expecting her?'

'If I had been, I wouldn't have been there,' he said curtly. 'As it was, I concluded the civilised thing to do was take her for a quick drink somewhere close at hand before escorting her politely out of my life. Which, by the way, is what I did. But not before you'd compared me to every reptile in the book and done your best to vanish from my life.'

'I'm sorry,' said Elf, meaning it.

'I should hope so. And now, Miss Makepeace, I don't want to hear one more word about Miranda, because I have someone much more important to discuss.' He crossed his arms on his chest.

'Who?' Elf eyed him doubtfully.

'A certain young lady called Elfriede, who's been driving me to the brink of murder for several weeks.' He pushed himself away from the door, and she watched the muscles pull tight across his thighs as he moved towards her. 'Where in hell did you get the ridiculous idea that I don't love you?'

Elf clutched at the collar of her blouse, pulling it up around her neck. Something that was part-hope and part-desperation swelled inside her. 'From you,' she replied. 'I got it from you. You said you wanted a nice, un-obtrusive wife—for your mother.'

'What?' Richard lifted his hand as if he wanted to hit something. Then, seeing her shrink back against the pillows, he swore softly and ran it through his hair. 'I suppose I asked for that,' he muttered.

'Mmm,' agreed Elf. 'You did. You've been driving me crazy for weeks too.'

'Good,' said Richard. He stared down at her, and gradually the look of strain she'd noticed earlier seemed to fade, and as he bent towards her his eyes started to gleam.

Elf swallowed, not trusting that gleam. But he only dropped on to the bed again and pulled her into his arms.

'Ouch,' said Elf, when the bump on her head collided with his chin.

He swore and laid her gently back on the pillows. 'Be careful with my favourite face,' he ordered. 'I won't have it looking like a grape.'

'Is it really your favourite face?' And was this really only a dream? Surely it had to be.

'Can you doubt it? I can't think of another face I could stand to see at breakfast every morning.'

Elf sat up again, swinging her feet to the floor and sitting beside him so she wouldn't have to look into his eyes. 'Every morning?' she asked cautiously, still not quite daring to believe.

'That's what I said.' He put his hands on her shoulders, turning her firmly to face him. 'I love you, Elf. Will you marry me? For at least the fourth time of asking?'

She heard the words, spoken quietly but with a gut-wrenching sincerity—words that she knew he had never expected to utter. She looked into the green eyes that were deep with a tenderness she had abandoned all hope of ever seeing there—and a feeling of peace grew inside her. She wasn't alone any more.

'I will,' she said softly, lifting a hand to touch his cheek, and even now not entirely convinced he wasn't a figment of concussion. But his skin was smooth, tough and incontrovertibly real. 'I was going to say "yes" that day you had the accident with the Range Rover. Even though I was sure you didn't love me. But I thought maybe in time...' She closed her eyes. 'In the end I—I changed my mind.'

'Why?' His voice was suddenly raw.

'Because I knew I wouldn't be able to bear being married to you if you didn't love me. And by then I was sure you weren't capable of anything more than affection. Later I almost changed it again, but I met Jean and she told me you weren't—well, being a hermit. There were calls from a Miss Kelsey, and somebody called Lady Keating —— '

'Elf,' said Richard, placing two fingers across her lips, 'Shut up.'

Elf shut up, and the man she loved enfolded her in his arms.

'That's better,' he said. 'Now, let's start at the beginning. First of all, and just to make things quite clear, when I marry it will be to suit myself, not my mother, much as I know she'll adore you. Secondly, Miss Kelsey and Lady Keating are strictly business. They're dress designers—long-time rivals, and sometimes they use my jewellery in their shows. Thirdly, if Jean told you I haven't been living the life of a hermit, I imagine all she meant was that I haven't given up on my friends. *Not* that I've been reincarnated as Don Juan.' He pulled her head on to his shoulder and ran his thumb gently along the back of her neck.

Elf rubbed her cheek against his soft white sweater. 'But you never told me you loved me,' she said quietly. 'Not until now —— '

'Dear God.' Richard pulled away from her. 'Elf...' He lowered his head, seemingly at a loss for words. When he looked up again she saw pain, and guilt, and a sort of yearning regret. 'Elf, I couldn't tell you I loved you, because it wasn't true. Not at first. Or if it was I was too stubborn or too stupid to accept it. After all, it was only eleven months since I'd lost Felicity.' He wiped a hand over his forehead and stood up, turning his back on her. 'You see, I spent nine years married to a woman who didn't love me, who never pretended to love me, and, although I came to terms with that, in the beginning I did hope— I tried damn hard...' He straightened his shoulders and started again. 'I'm not saying it was Felicity's fault. Maybe I could have done more. She had the occasional bodily need which I satisfied, but her whole life had always been wrapped up in horses. She wasn't capable of caring much for a mere man. I'm a competent horseman, but I'm not obsessed by them, and Felicity had no patience with anything less...'

'Richard,' said Elf gently. 'What are you trying to say?'

He walked over to the window, pressed his palms flat on the sill, and stared down into the street. 'I'm trying to say,' he replied, in a voice that gave nothing away, 'that even once I realised I wanted to marry you for reasons that were neither convenient nor lustful——'

'When was that?' she interrupted softly.

'Somewhere around the time Mr Busby threatened to eject you for being drunk and disorderly, I think. Although I *should* have known when the ship caught fire, and the only thing I could think of was you.' He paused, and then went on quietly, 'I found it impossible to tell you I loved you, Elf, because I still couldn't quite believe I did. Or that you did. A long time ago I'd had those words thrown back in my face, and I've never forgotten how it felt. I stopped expecting love after that.'

'Poor Richard,' said Elf softly.

'Poor?' He threw his head back. 'I didn't feel deprived, Elf. In fact I felt I'd learned a useful lesson. But perhaps I should have known it was flawed when I found myself willing—almost relieved—to accept Jerry's estimate of my behaviour and ——'

'Give me another chance,' said Elf drily.

He swung round to face her, his lips parted in a rueful grin. 'Precisely.'

She shook her head, knowing that this time he was laughing with her and not at her. 'I don't understand how a marriage between two people who didn't believe in love could have lasted so long,' she told him, softening the words with a smile.

He frowned. 'I suppose that's *why* it lasted in a way. Felicity was perfectly content, and I convinced myself I was too. And when she died I missed her—more than I'd ever imagined I could. Then, after all those years, I found you again...'

'Oh,' cried Elf, holding out her arms. 'Oh, Richard. I loved you all along, I think. But I didn't understand. You needed to hear those words as much as I did —— '

'Everybody does, if I'd only known it,' he said gruffly. He crossed the room in two strides, and swept her on to her feet. Briefly their eyes met, soft and hungry with love. Then they were locked together in the embrace they had both been waiting for all of their lives.

A long time later, when Elf had said 'ouch' rather convincingly for the third time, Richard let her go and sat down in one of the dusky-pink chairs. He shook his head. 'How can I possibly marry a woman who says "ouch" every time I make love to her?' he groaned.

'Changed your mind?' asked Elf, grinning.

'Certainly not. Why would I turn down the opportunity to marry a lady who reminds me of my misspent youth—frequently—gets sick into flower bowls, calls me a toad, needs putting to bed with promising regularity, and says "ouch"...?'

'Yes, I know. Every time you make love to me. I do see that must make me irresistible.' She held out her hands to him and he pulled her on to his knee. 'I won't say "ouch" if you try again,' she suggested, pushing her fingers up under his sweater.

For a moment she thought he was going to take her at her word. But instead he drew a deep breath that forced his taut muscles to relax, and kissed her thoroughly but with an air of restraint.

'You've had an eventful day and that's a nasty bump on your head,' he said when he had finished. 'I would enjoy nothing better than to make passionate love to you for the next twelve hours, but I'm afraid we'll have to move that further down the agenda. Right now what you need is rest.'

'I couldn't possibly rest,' she said, trailing a thumb slowly along his thigh.

'Keep that up and I'll be giving you the cold shower I could do with myself,' he said grimly, removing the hand and scooping her up in his arms. 'So be good and rest—for a while anyway. After that you'll need to eat—and then we'll see...'

'I couldn't —— '

'Yes, you could.' He tipped her on to the bed.

And he was right. She could. In a very little while she was asleep.

When she awoke the light was fading outside the window and deep blue shadows filled the room. There was a vase of yellow roses beside the bed.

As she lay blinking in the half-light and listening to the low drone of a plane overhead, the bathroom door was flung open and Richard came out, drying his hair with one hand and holding a pair of trousers in the other. He was dressed, though Elf wasn't sure dressed was the right word, in a brief white towel with the hotel's name emblazoned across one corner.

'You shouldn't look like that,' she muttered in a choked voice.

Richard tossed the trousers on to the bed and picked up his shirt. 'Why shouldn't I look like this?'

'Because I've already been hit on the head once today, and it's bad for my blood-pressure, that's why.'

He laughed and sat down beside her. 'You're obviously feeling better,' he remarked.

What she was actually feeling was an overpowering desire to touch the golden flesh of his thighs, to run her fingers through the silky blond hair covering his chest . . . but, knowing him, he would probably say she ought to rest some more—or get some food in her stomach.

It wasn't food she was hungry for, and to take her mind off the seductive proximity of his thighs she asked quickly, 'Where did the roses come from?'

'I had them sent up. Do you like roses, daffodil?'

'I love them.' Elf picked up the vase and buried her nose in the fragrant blossoms. 'Thank you. Roses are my favourite thing.'

'*Roses* are your favourite thing.' Richard sighed. 'And I was optimistic enough to think I was.'

'Well, not my *very* favourite,' said Elf, with a smile that made him want to make love to her right there on the hotel-beige carpet.

Because it might still be too soon, all he did was ruffle his hand through her curls and give her a smart pat on her jeans.

'Oh, Richard.' Elf lifted her nose from the soft petals. 'Oh, Richard, I was so—so alone, so sure I always would be, and now I'm— I'm...' Her voice broke. 'I'm so happy. It feels like—oh, I don't know.' She waved the vase at him. 'Like —— '

'Like roses,' he finished drily, as a thorn speared him neatly on the chin.

Elf waved the bouquet again. Richard grabbed her wrist. 'Heaven help me,' he muttered, rolling his eyes at the ceiling. 'If my wife can't even handle roses without blazing a trail of destruction...' He stopped, and finished in quite a different voice, 'I can hardly wait to find out what other surprises you'll spring on me.'

'I can handle roses perfectly well,' said Elf, clasping the vase to her chest. She smiled. 'And I can hardly wait either.'

Richard stood up, laughing. Then he bent down, removed the flowers and swung her into the air.

'Put me down,' she laughed. 'Richard...'

He put her down. 'I love you, Elf,' he murmured against her hair.

'I love you too—ouch!'

Richard released her abruptly and muttered a few crudely explicit words. 'I give up,' he groaned. 'I adore you, my beloved, but I'm damned if I'm going to spend the rest of my life with a woman whose only term of endearment is "ouch".'

'I stepped on a thorn,' replied Elf, in an aggrieved voice. 'One of the rose-buds fell out.'

Richard bent to pick it up. 'The point is —' he began.

Elf removed the bud from his hand and placed it carefully in the vase with the others. 'The point is in my foot,' she told him glumly, sinking to the floor to remove the thorn.

Richard muttered something she didn't catch as he waited for her to complete the operation. Then he reached down to pull her on to her feet, his eyes so filled with love that the moment he held out his arms Elf stepped into them.

'And don't you dare say "ouch",' he warned her as she opened her mouth.

Elf didn't, and Richard need not have worried because it was a very long time before either of them said anything at all.